A SAVAGE'S PRINCESS

RAYA REIGN

TEXT UCP TO 22828 TO SUBSCRIBE TO OUR MAILING LIST
If you would like to join our team, submit the first 3-4 chapters of your completed manuscript to
Submissions@UrbanChaptersPublications.com

SEMAJ

A guy moaning was my favorite thing to hear. All a man had to do was moan around me, and that would get me wetter than the ocean. No foreplay needed.

Marcus knew that.

He would start at my feet. Putting my toes in his mouth and moaning like they were the best thing he'd ever tasted. Then, he'd move up to my legs, carefully kissing each leg until he reached my thighs — one of my hot spots. He would take his time groping, licking, and kissing all over my thighs. He probably thought that was the thing that turned me on the most, but nope. That deep moan that came from the back of his throat had already done it for me.

After he was done caressing my things, he'd move up to my woman hood, planting soft kisses on it, making me quiver, whimper, and grab a hold of his dreads that he'd been growing his entire life. Usually, he'd assault my vagina with his tongue for about thirty minutes, but this time was different.

He came up and looked at me with a wicked look in his eye, which made my eyebrow raise.

"What?" I asked, watching him slide off the bed.

"I got an idea," he said as he left the room. He was gone before I could ask him what was going on, but he returned even quicker with a small bottle of Hennessy. He knew I wasn't a drinker, so I wasn't quite sure what he was going to do with that.

"Marcus, you know I don't—"

"Hush," he said, as he twisted the top off.

He started by pouring a small amount on my stomach. He slurped it up, making chills run down my spine. Once Marcus knew that I liked it, he kept doing it. I didn't have a problem with it. It was a change of pace from what we usually do.

I couldn't help but prop up on my elbows when I noticed him moving lower and lower. I mean, the gesture was sexy and everything, but I think I'd had enough. I wasn't a doctor or anything, but I was almost certain you shouldn't pour liquor in—

"Oh my God, Marcus!" I screamed, jumping straight off the bed.

"What? What's wrong?"

"This mess burns! It burns bad! Why would you even think that pouring this in my pussy was a good idea?!"

This was a pain I'd never felt before. I didn't know what to do, but I just needed the burning sensation to stop. I ran straight for the bathroom, leaving Marcus in the room looking stupid.

In the bathroom, I turned the water on in the bathtub, but I couldn't figure out a way to lay under the faucet so I could let the water run on it. I don't want to sound dramatic or anything, but I really felt like I was dying.

"You okay? Do you need anything?" Marcus asked rushing into the bathroom now with some boxers on.

I cut my eyes at him. Right now, he was the last person I wanted to see.

"Take me to the hospital, Marcus."

"So... You want me to take you home?" Marcus asked after just driving in silence. We'd just spent four hours at the emergency room because I thought I was about to die. The doctor told me I'd be okay, but it's possible for me to have a yeast infection. I didn't even look in Marcus' direction.

"Yes. Take me home. I'd like to go to sleep in my own bed, thank you." I flipped my hair off my shoulder and crossed my arms. I was so embarrassed. My vagina was in so much pain earlier, I could barely walk. I had people looking at me like I was crazy all because Marcus wanted to be dumb.

"I'm sorry, Semaj. I didn't know that would happen. I just wanted to spice things up... I know you probably get tired of doing the same position all the time and—"

"Just please stop talking. I don't wanna talk about it right now."

Marcus only liked missionary. Sometimes, he'd let me on top, but it would never last long. He didn't like it. He hated it from the back, and that was the one position I liked the most. The only good thing about sex with Marcus was he waited for me to have an orgasm before he had his. Also, he knew exactly what to do with his tongue.

If I ever complained about the sex, Marcus would act like he didn't hear me. It got to the point where I just stopped saying anything about it. He wasn't even my boyfriend. I scoffed thinking about it.

Marcus claimed he wasn't the relationship type. He claimed a relationship would slow him down and make him lose focus. He was a lawyer, so I didn't know what the hell he was going to lose focus on. I used to press the issue, but now, I don't see the point. He doesn't want me as a girlfriend. He just wants to be able to fuck me whenever he pleases.

"Hmph," I snorted, crossing my arms. "Lesson learned. Don't try this with your other women."

"Come on, Semaj. Don't start this again. How many times do I have to tell you that I don't have any other bitches? When you gonna grow the hell up and stop worrying about other women?"

"Excuse me?" I said, with my voice nearly going up an octave. "I know I may question a lot because first off, I have the right to, but let's get one thing straight," I pointed a finger in his face. "Semaj will never be worried about another woman. I don't care how much money she has, or how much—"

"I thought you said you didn't wanna talk? Why can't we just ride in silence?" he glanced in my direction before he quickly averted his attention back to the dark road.

"I didn't wanna talk, but now I do! I know you're fucking other women because I saw the condom rappers in the trash earlier! We don't use condoms! Ever!"

He pulled an annoyed hand down his face. "Why you always have to do this? Why ruin a good night with your insecurities?"

"A good night?! There is nothing *good* about this night at all! You almost burned my vagina off, Marcus! Now, you're sitting here lying to me when I know the truth! You think I'm stupid? You think just because I'm twenty-two that I'm stupid? Yeah, I'm young, but I'm definitely not dumb." I crossed my arms again and waited for his response. Instead of responding like I thought he would, he just laughed.

"You know what else you'll never be, Semaj?" he asked, with a slow lick of his lips.

"What?" I questioned, with my eyes narrowing.

"My woman." The laugh that followed his statement was a cold one. He even threw his head back like he'd just told the funniest joke.

"Let me out of this car," I said quietly, but loud enough for him to hear me.

"What? No. I'm not letting you out. It's dark and we're almost to your place. Just sit there until—"

"I said let me out, Marcus! Let me out of this fucking car before I jump out of it!" Now, that's something I would never do. I would never risk my life by jumping out of a moving car, but he didn't know that. "I'm not playing with you!"

He slammed on the breaks, almost causing me to hit my head on the dashboard, and I snatched my purse. I popped the door open, stepped out the car, then smoothed my skirt down.

"Good bye, Marcus." I said, then slammed the door as hard as I could.

There were three blocks to get to my house from where I was at, and suddenly, I regretted wearing these heels.

"Great," I muttered, watching Marcus turn his car around and leave. I was shocked he actually left me out here alone, but at the same time, I wasn't. Marcus was an asshole, clearly. I wasn't sure why I was still wasting my time with him.

I shook my head and began my journey home. I hated the dark. I felt like someone was always watching me. I could've easily called an Uber to come get me, but I was too afraid to just stand out here waiting for them to come get me. I had a small thing of pepper spray on my keychain, and I had a small pocket knife in my purse. Hopefully, I wouldn't have to use it, but it made me feel a little better knowing I had it.

I hadn't even made it halfway down the street and my feet were already hurting. I thought about taking my shoes off, and just walking home barefoot, but that would do more damage to my feet, and Marcus loved how pretty and groomed I kept them.

Honestly, I think he had a foot fetish. He would always put my toes in his mouth like it was nothing. He never had a problem with it.

I couldn't believe I was walking home, scared out of my mind, and I was still thinking about Marcus and what he liked. I shouldn't care about any of that because he barely cared about me or my feelings.

I quickly pulled out my phone and called my best friend. I felt like maybe if I talked to someone on my walk home, I'd feel a little better.

"Bitch, where the hell you at? I been at your house waiting for you for hours. Damn. What if I wanted to have a girl's night or something?" Trinity snapped when she answered the phone.

"Sorry," I huffed. "I was at the emergency room."

"What? Why? You okay? Why didn't you call me sooner?!"

I sighed because I didn't want to talk about it. "Marcus decided he wanted to spice things up in the bedroom and... long story short, he poured liquor in my vagina and almost gave me a chemical burn. Now, I'm walking home. I'm like—"

"Hold on, what?" she yelled with laughter. "He did what?! Why did he think that was a good idea? I swear, for that nigga to be a lawyer, he's dumb as shit. Why— hold the hell on. Bitch did you just say you were walking?"

"Yes. We got into an argument and I told him to let me out of his car before I jumped out of it. He let me out, then drove off. I picked the wrong day to wear heels," I sighed, glancing behind me because I still had that feeling that someone was watching me.

"Mannnn," she groaned. "See, this is why I always tell you to leave that nigga alone. He ain't shit and he's never gonna be shit. What man would let you walk home in the dark like this? The next time I see him I'm punching him straight in the mouth for being a dumb ass." I could hear a lot of shuffling going on from her side of the phone.

"He's not a nigga," I whispered because I hated that word. I hated saying it, I hated when Trinity said it, and I hated being called one. The word was just so ugly.

"Girl," she laughed. "Yes the fuck he is. A dumb ass nigga at that. I really wish you would leave him alone. Why do you let him treat you like this? You're better than that, Semaj."

I rolled my eyes because we had this conversation at least once a week. "We're not even together. It's not that big of a deal."

"Umm, yes the fuck it is. That nigga got you walking in the dark by yourself. You're a woman, Semaj. Niggas take advantage of that shit. You can't fight, and you look like it. A nigga cold be watching you right now, ready to pounce on you like a—"

"Trinity?!" I squealed, turning to look behind me again. "I'm already paranoid out here. You're making it worse."

"It's okay boo, because I'm already in the car on the way to you. I just couldn't believe this shit. You need to do better at selecting your men."

I sighed to myself. I couldn't even bring myself to say anything back to her because she was right. Everything she said about Marcus was the truth.

"Is this you right here? Walking in the middle of the damn street?" she asked, as the headlights of her car blinded me.

"Yes," I said, squinting my eyes. She wasted no time pulling up next to me. I quickly got in the passenger seat and let out a sigh of relief.

"Thank you for coming to rescue me. I don't know what I'd do if you weren't here."

"You would've walked your ass home in the dark," she laughed, causing me to roll my eyes.

I decided not to respond to her. I really just wanted to get home and act like this night never even happened.

"What's up, Semaj?" I heard from behind me. I didn't need to turn around to know who it was. Instead, I snapped my head in Trinity's direction. The guilt was already playing out on her face.

"Before you cuss me out, just know this wasn't my plan. He wouldn't leave and followed me to the car. That nigga scares me, so I decided to keep my mouth shut. I didn't wanna get shot!" she said as I turned my head to look at Tristan who was sitting in the back seat.

"Why are you here?" I asked with my lips tight. Couldn't stand him. Shit, I couldn't stand my daddy's side of the family period. I didn't even claim Tristan as my cousin.

"You know I wouldn't be here if it wasn't serious. Don't nobody like dealing with your wannabe white ass, anyway," he chuckled.

"Okay?! And I don't like dealing with y'all ghetto—"

"Your dad's dead." he said easily, making me snap my mouth shut.

"Huh?" I heard him perfectly. I just wanted him to repeat it.

"He's dead, Semaj. Got killed. Shot in the chest. That's why I'm here."

I didn't know what to say. My daddy was never in my life. Back before my mom died, he would come around maybe once or twice a month, but once I hit middle school, that ended completely. I always felt like he didn't want me. He probably thought I was gonna grow up to act just like my mom since she was a… crack head.

My mom died right after I graduated high school. She overdosed. I was sad, but I expected it. When I got old enough to know about my mom and her addiction, I just always told myself that she would die from it one day, and I was right.

So, now here I am at age twenty-two with no parents. I never expected that this is how my life would be at this age. I wasn't even twenty-five yet.

"When's the funeral?" I asked, when we finally pulled up in the driveway.

"In two days. But, that's not all I'm here for. We need to talk," he looked in Trinity's direction. "In private."

I nodded, then slowly got out the car. I could feel a pain forming in my chest, but I quickly tried to shake it off. I hated crying in front of people, and I damn sure wasn't about to do it in front of Tristan.

He followed close behind me as opened the front door, then started up the stairs. It sounded like he was purposely stomping up my stairs like a mad ass teenager, and that made me stop in my tracks.

"Tristan, can you please not stomp up my stairs? It's really annoying."

He smacked his lips. "You'll find any little reason to talk shit, Semaj. Hurry the hell up so I can tell you everything you need to know." That made me raise a brow. Everything I needed to know about what?

When we finally made it to my room, he closed the door behind him. I stood in front of him with my arms crossed, waiting for him to say what he needed to say.

"Your pops left everything in his will to you," he said, running a hand down his face. "Everything."

"What? Everything like that? He didn't have shit!"

He let out a small laugh. "Nah. There's a lot of shit you don't know about your dad."

"Like what?" I lifted an eyebrow.

"Just be up early tomorrow, aight? I'm coming to get you. I got some shit to show you." He turned to leave before I could respond to him. I didn't know what to say after that.

"What the hell just happened?"

TRISTAN

No one liked dealing with Semaj. She'd always acted stuck up and boujiee since we were younger, but once her mom died, that shit got worse.

Dwayne getting killed was unexpected. That shit shocked everyone. Dwayne was untouchable in the streets. Everyone knew him, and everyone respected him. We couldn't understand who would want to kill him, but best believe we were gonna find out.

I remember him always talking about Semaj and how he wanted to make things right with her. He thought she hated his ass because that's how she acted. She never came around for birthdays, family functions, or anything. Shit was sad as fuck that they didn't get to mend their relationship before he died.

I told Semaj to be ready by the time I got to her crib, but I should've known that wasn't gonna happen. I'd been sitting out here for almost an hour waiting on her ass. I thought about calling her, and telling her to hurry the fuck up, but instead, I started blowing my horn.

It was early as fuck and I knew I was probably pissing the neighbors off, but I didn't give a fuck. She needed to bring her ass because I was tired of sitting out here.

About five minutes of me blowing the horn, and the front door flew open. she stormed out with her face twisted up.

"Tristan, what the hell is wrong with you?!" she snapped when she pulled the door open. "I have neighbors!"

I shrugged and started the car. "I don't give a fuck about your damn neighbors. I told you to be ready when I got here. I see ain't nothing changed about your terrible listening skills."

She smacked her lips. "Fuck you. I told you it was too early when you called!"

"And I told you I didn't give a fuck. We got shit to do today. Time is money."

She sat back in the seat and crossed her arms. I was sitting there wondering why the hell she was dressed like she was about to go to a job interview.

She had on a white blouse with a burgundy blazer and some black dress pants. Her hair was jet black and long as fuck. I wasn't sure if that was all her hair or not, but the shit was long. Then, on top of her outfit, she was wearing heels.

"Man, why the hell you dressed like you're about to give a speech? The fuck you—"

"I'm sorry that I like to look presentable when I leave the house. I didn't know my outfit was going to bother you so much." She flipped her hair off her shoulder and looked at me.

"Yeah, I feel that, but you look like—"

"I look like I'm minding my business, Tristan. You should do the same. You don't see me saying anything about your nappy ass hair, those ugly ass tattoos, or the fact that you always smell like pot when you come around."

"Pot?" I laughed. "That's what you call it?"

She nodded. "That's what it is. Either way, it stinks, and makes you act stupid. Don't know how people smoke it all the time,"

"Clearly, *you* don't know how to act when you smoke."

"I don't smoke," she said firmly. "I don't smoke anything. Not even cigarettes. That's really disgusting."

"How you feeling?" I asked, changing the subject.

She gave me a half shrug. "I mean, I don't know. Me and my daddy didn't have the best relationship—"

"Yeah, but he was trying to change that."

She waved me off. "That man hated me. He probably hated that I was even born."

"Is that what you made yourself believe? That nigga loved you. Why the hell you think he left everything to you? That nigga had a whole wife and didn't leave her shit,"

"What do you mean by he left everything to me? What exactly did he have? I know damn well he doesn't have any money because when my mom would call him, asking for money, he would never send it. He would never help her with me. We struggled because—"

"Your moms was a crack head, Semaj. Your dad always sent money, your mom just smoked that shit up."

She shook her head, probably because she didn't want to believe it. "No, she didn't."

"I promise you she did. I've been around plenty of crackheads. I know—"

"Okay, well my mom was different. Yeah, she was a crackhead, but she took care of me. You can't tell me no different."

"Aight, Semaj. You got that shit. I won't say shit else about it. I'll let you figure everything out."

"Thanks."

The rest of the ride was quiet. She didn't have shit to say to me and I didn't have shit to say to her. I hated to say this, but I liked her a lot better when we were kids. Now, she acted like she was too good for everyone.

"You don't live around here, do you?" she asked, looking around.

"Nah,"

"Whew, good. Why are we even on this side of town? It's making me uncomfortable." She locked her door as I laughed to myself.

"Do you act like this on purpose or what?"

Her brows came together. "Act like what?"

"Like you wasn't born and raised in the hood. Like ya' mama wasn't out here sucking dick behind dumpsters for drugs." I watched her as her facial expression changed. She didn't know what to say.

"Well," she started, while flipping her hair. "I'd rather have a mama who was a crackhead and still tried to care for me instead of a mama who acts like I don't exist. She even had another son who she treats like gold. How is your mom, Tristan? Oh wait, you don't know because she doesn't answer when you call."

For a second, I wanted to stop the car and push her ass out of it, but I couldn't. There was business that needed to be handled first.

"You real funny," I let her know. I even laughed a little to hide how angry I really was.

My mom wasn't shit. there wasn't any other way to say it. Yeah, she had me when she was young, but once my pops decided he didn't wanna be with her anymore, she decided she didn't wanna be my mom anymore.

As a young nigga, that shit hurt. I could never bring myself to understand why she was treating me like I wasn't shit. Once I let my pops know how my mom was treating me, that nigga was heated.

I swear, he cussed her out for about an hour, calling her every damn name in the book. After that, he made me move in with him. My mom didn't give a fuck, though. She was just happy I was out her house.

"Don't come for me, Tristan. I'll hurt your feelings and you know it. That's why you're sitting over there about to cry now," she said as we pulled into the parking lot of a car dealership.

"You got it Semaj." I nodded, getting out the car. "Now bring yo ass."

She gave me a weird look before she got out the car, adjusted her pants, then walked her extra ass around the car to stand next to me.

"You buying a car?" she questioned, following behind me. "Why are we here?"

"Hush. You talking too damn much." She muttered something under her breath that I didn't give a fuck about.

"I was wondering when you were gonna bring yo' bright ass in here, nigga." Daren said as we dapped each other up. He was the manager here. Me and that nigga went way back.

"Yeah, just here to introduce you to your new boss and shit." I glanced at Semaj who gave me a weird look.

"What? We didn't talk about this," she tried to whisper, but was still loud as hell.

"Well, your dad left everything to you, including his businesses." I let her know, watching her eyes widen in shock.

She started shaking her head. "No. I don't want it. First off, we're in the ghetto. Who wants to—"

"Ayo, chill the fuck out. You really getting on my nerves with this shit. instead of complaining about where the place is located, you should be happy that you never have to work again."

She quickly looked around the building, still shaking her head. There wasn't shit she could do about it. This shit was hers now.

"So, I own a business now?" she asked, looking back and forth between me and Daren.

"A business?" I chuckled. "You really didn't know shit about your daddy, huh? Come on, I got some more shit to show you."

So, after showing Semaj the car dealership, the barber shop, and soul food restaurant she now owned, we sat in my car with her staring blankly out the window.

"Why would he do this?" he asked, quietly. She'd been asking the same question over and over since we got back in the car.

"I guess this was his way of making things up to you."

"I don't want it. I don't want any of this. I don't have what it takes to own a business. I'm in school to be a lawyer, Tristan."

I nodded. "Yeah. I know what the hell you're in school for." She made sure to let everyone know why she was in college. She always let people know when they never asked.

"Like, who the hell does he think I am? Why couldn't he just leave me money or something?"

"He did. Left you money, his houses, and his businesses. Any normal person would be grateful, but you've always been—"

"Houses?! How many did he have? I'm gonna have to pay the bills now? Are you serious?"

I sighed loudly. "You complain a lot. You just got rich without having to work for it, but you're over here bitching and shit. That's annoying, Semaj."

"What? I got rich because my dad got killed. Why would I be happy about any of this? There's more to life than just money! I don't have any parents, Tristan! I'm all alone out here now. When I have kids, they're not gonna have grandparents!"

I didn't respond to her as I started the car and pulled out the parking lot. I knew she was grieving and shit, and this was a fucked up situation, but I was tired of being around her. She was fucking with my inner peace, and I was gonna end up saying something that would hurt her feelings.

"You hungry?" I asked, glancing over at her as she texted on her phone. I wasn't used to girls like Semaj. All the woman I fucked with were hood bitches. Born and raised in the hood and proud of that shit.

Whenever I was with one, the first thing they would ask was for me to buy them some food. Shit, most the time, they were begging me to take them shopping. They always wanted me to spend money on them, but Semaj hasn't asked for shit since we been around each other.

It could've been because we were cousins, and she didn't feel right asking me for anything, or it could've been because she didn't really know shit about me. She didn't even know I had money.

"I am, actually. Take me to Arby's, please." She blew out a breath and dropped her phone in the cup holder.

"Arby's? Man, don't nobody eat that nasty shit."

"Well, I do. And, it's not nasty."

"Yes the fuck it is. You don't want McDonalds? Them fried sounding real good right now." I hadn't ate shit all day. I woke up and went straight to Semaj's crib.

"No, I don't want McDonalds! The food is fake. I don't see how they're still in business. I can't—"

"Shut up, Semaj. We're eating McDonalds. End of discussion."

She smacked her lips and sat back in her seat. "I'm not eating McDonalds. I'll just eat when I get home," I could hear the attitude in her voice, but I didn't care about it. I offered her ungrateful ass food, and she didn't want it. That shit ain't my problem.

After I stopped at McDonalds and listened to Semaj talk shit to some nigga on the phone, I finally dropped her back off at her place. There was still a lot of shit I needed to show her, but I'd do all that after the funeral.

"I'll see you later," she said, popping her door open to get out.

"Aye, you own a gun?"

She twisted her face up. "Do I look like I own a gun, Tristan? Do I look like I even know what to do with one?"

"Man, it was a simple yes or no question. All you had to do was say no. You always got some extra shit to say."

"Why does it matter if I own a gun or not?"

I chuckled as I looked at her. "You're gonna need one."

3

TRINITY

"He had four houses," Semaj sighed as she took another sip of wine. She slumped into the couch like it was the end of the world.

But me? I couldn't understand why she was sad. This bitch just got her entire life upgraded without having to lift a finger. I'd be jumping around right now and acting like I didn't have any damn sense.

"Okay?" I said, sitting down on the couch next to her. "Bitch, you got options now. What the hell you complaining about? You always find a way to find the bad in things."

"Tristan said the same thing. I just don't understand how I'm supposed to be happy at a time like this... I'm sure his wife is mad that he gave me everything."

"Duh, but who gives a fuck. Bitch, you got money now. You got money, businesses, and some houses. We should be turning up right now. Drinking because this shit is great. But instead, you're drinking because you're sad. Such a weirdo."

"Celebrate? Celebrate my dad's death? That's not something that I wanna do. I'm still coming to terms that my daddy is actually gone. I can't even remember the last time I talked to him. I just can't even believe this shit."

"Well, is Marcus going to the funeral with you?"

"Girl, no. He's gonna be out of town for business the day of the funeral."

I rolled my eyes as I brought the cup up to my lips. "He's probably gonna be with his wife and kids."

"Why do you always do that? Why do you always say he's with another woman? I know for a fact he's not married."

"Do you?" I asked, lifting a brow. "You've been messing around with him for how long? And you two still aren't together? Nah, Semaj. You the side bitch."

I couldn't stand Marcus. I didn't trust his ass, and the way he treated Semaj? That shit just made me hate him even more. I wanted her to leave his ass alone because she was always in her feelings about him, but she acted like she would die if she was to stop messing around with his ass.

Semaj wasn't ugly. She was actually one of the prettiest friends I had. With her light brown skin, banging ass body that she never showed off, and the way she kept her hair done? Any nigga would be lucky to have her ass, but she didn't realize it.

"Don't say that!" she snapped. "I'm not a side bitch. Me and him aren't even together. He's not ready for a relationship, and I'm okay with that. I don't understand why that's such a problem for you."

"Because you're always acting like you're about to die when y'all argue or something. Nigga never has time for you, girl that man has even left you while y'all were on a date. He didn't even tell you he was leaving, he just did it. Like it was nothing. He's a whole clown, but I guess that's what you like."

She nodded. "Well, how are you and your boyfriend, since you wanna be all up in my love life? I haven't heard you talking about him lately like you usually do."

I fought the urge to roll my eyes. I didn't even wanna think about my boyfriend, Antonio, who was also Semaj's cousin. When I first saw his fine, chocolate ass, I fell in love. Semaj told me not to mess with him because he wasn't shit, but I didn't listen.

There's been so much drama in my life ever since me and Antonio got together. I lost count of women who call me, coming to me as a woman. I've had my tires flattened, car scratched up, and even had them break one of my windows. I was sick and tired of it. I was sick of getting cheated on, and I was sick of getting lied to. So, a couple days ago, I left him. He's been begging for me to take him back, but nah. I wasn't falling for his lies again.

"I don't have a boyfriend anymore." I said, easily.

"What? And when were you gonna tell me? You were just gonna sit here and act like y'all two were still together?"

"I'm not acting like shit. I got tired of him constantly lying to me, tired of getting cheated on... I'm done with that nigga." I said it, but I wasn't gonna sit here and lie like I hadn't been missing his annoying ass.

"You sure? You didn't sound to certain about that, Trin."

"I'm positive."

"The men in my family are trash. All of them."

"You know, it's crazy that you say that because yesterday, Tristan was trying to get at me like I wasn't with y'alls cousin." I said, with a light laugh.

"Really? Maybe he was just playing. You know how he is."

I shook my head. "No. He wasn't playing. Nigga was begging for my number. Tristan is cute and all, but I'd never mess with him."

Or would I? I remember meeting Tristan a long time ago when we were younger. He was always playing basketball at the park, and looking delicious.

He'd always been tall, and had that small curly fro, but now that he was grown, had that nice ass body, tattoos, and that full beard? He looked like my next meal.

"Trinity? What you over there dreaming about? You're thinking about Tristan, aren't you?"

"What? No. Mind your damn business."

She shook her head while letting out a small sigh. "Please don't go from one of my cousins to another one. I'm begging you."

I dismissively waved her off. "Girl, shut up. I don't want any more men from your family. Them niggas don't know how to act."

"Yeah, you said the same thing about Antonio, but you decided to get with him, anyway."

"Okay, but now I'm not with him. I'm fine with being single. I might even find me a couple new niggas to play with. I'm not sure yet."

She shrugged as she looked down at her cup. "If that's what you wanna do, Trin. Men are the least of my worries right now. I'm just trying to figure out how I'm going to run three businesses by myself. I'm not ready for any of this."

"Semaj, shut the hell up. You're always finding something to stress over. Tomorrow, after the funeral, we're turning the fuck up. I'm taking you to a club and you're gonna shake your ass on some niggas you'll never see again." I did a little dance in my seat because the thought excited me. I hadn't been to a club in a long time. Antonio would never let me go unless he was coming with me, and half the time, I didn't want his annoying ass coming.

He was a vibe killer, and he always wanted to control everything. He would get mad when I'd have fun with my friends, so he always wanted to leave early. He hated when I got drunk, and he damn sure hated when I shook my ass.

Hell no," Semaj said, with her face twisted up. "I'm definitely not—"

"Umm, yes the fuck you are. We're going out tomorrow even if I have to drag your ass. You're gonna get cute, then you're gonna get drunk, and I can't wait."

"So, we're celebrating my dad's death?"

Girl, ain't like you talked to the nigga, anyway.

"No, don't think of it like that. We're celebrating new beginnings. My bitch is rich now. We definitely have to celebrate this."

She was still shaking her head, but at this point, I didn't care anymore. I was gonna force her ass out tomorrow and there wasn't shit she could do about it.

"I'm really not ready to go to this funeral. They're always so sad," she said, finally finishing her drink.

"Semaj, what funeral have you been to that was happy?"

"I just would rather have him cremated. Why don't I have a say so in this? I mean, I am his only child." She had a point, but she never came around. They were probably feeling some type of way about Semaj.

"It's okay because at the end of the day, you're the one who got everything. So really, it's fuck them anyway."

She rolled her eyes and stood up. "You know what? There's just way too much going on right now. My brain hurts and I'm tired. I'm going to sleep. You can stay if you want." She walked away before I could respond to her.

I thought about staying at her place and drinking the rest of her wine, but I decided against it. I needed to be getting ready for the funeral in the morning. I was dreading it because I knew I was gonna cry, and I hated crying in front of people.

As I stood to leave, I felt my phone began to ring in my back pocket. I wasn't even a little surprised that Antonio was calling. He made sure to call me every hour when we were broken up.

"What nigga?" I answered as I slid in the driver's seat of my car.

"Where you at? I'm tryna come see you." I instantly rolled my eyes.

"I'm somewhere minding my business, Antonio. I don't wanna see you. Go see your other girlfriend."

"I tried, but she's busy tonight," he laughed. The fucking nerve of this nigga.

"Bye, Antonio. Delete my number."

"Wait, nah, nah, nah. I'm tryna talk to you. You at home?"

I smacked my lips. "Talk to me for what? Ain't shit to talk about, Antonio."

"I'm tryna talk about us, baby. Don't try to act like you don't miss a nigga. You know—"

"Nigga, I don't miss you! I'm doing perfectly fine without seeing your lying ass face or your dumb ass voice."

"Man, shut that dumb shit up. We need to talk in person. I'm about to pull up, aight?"

"No—" He hung up before I could finish my sentence. "Mannn, what the fuck?" I groaned, then tossed my phone in the other seat.

Antonio always did shit like this. Whenever we broke up, he'd give me a couple days, then he'd just show up to my apartment to "talk" but, it'd always end with me on all fours, screaming his name while he hit it from the back.

This night was no different. He came to my apartment looking good enough to eat. He had a fresh cut. His outfit was looking nice, and he looked even better with that toothpick dangling from his lips, and his hands casually in his pockets. He was leaning up against his car when I pulled up and I couldn't help but to roll my eyes.

I hated this nigga. I hated how dumb I was over his ass. I hated how weak I always got when he was around, and I mostly hated how he wouldn't keep his nasty ass dick in his pants.

"I did good today," he smiled as I walked past him. "I didn't break in yo' shit even though I wanted to."

I scoffed. "Oh, gee thanks, nigga."

"Where you coming from? Another nigga's house?"

"Does it matter?" I muttered, unlocking the door.

"Hell yeah, it matters! I'm not about to eat yo' pussy if you let another nigga up in that shit."

I chuckled lightly as I sat my keys on the counter, then turned to look at him. "You're not eating my pussy regardless. Fuck you thought?"

"But, I am," he nodded.

"But you're not."

"That's what you think, shawty."

I sighed loudly. "So, what did you want to talk about? Why are you here, all up in my personal space?"

"Because, I miss you. You know how hard it is sleeping in my big ass bed alone?"

"Antonio, shut the fuck up. You weren't thinking about me when you were out there sticking your dick in anything that smiles at you." I folded my arms and watched him watch me. Why did all the fine niggas have to be so damn stupid?

"What? I'm always thinking about you, girl. Always thinking about that big ole booty and them small ass titties." He took a step closer, then pulled my body to his.

"Boy, get off me. you came over here to talk, why you got your hands all over me?"

"Damn, so I can't touch you now? I can't touch my girl—"

"I'm not your girl! You want these trashy ass bitches that's always fucking my car up. I really wish you wouldn't have brought your ass over here. We don't have shit to talk about." I took a step away from him.

He thought that he could just show up, talk me out of my panties, then I would just forgive him? Yeah, that's usually how it went, but I was tired of it. I was trying to break that cycle.

Even though my brain wanted to break the cycle, my vagina had a mind of her own.

So, here I am, lying beside him in my bed, naked. I felt disgusting that I'd just had sex with him, but the shit was amazing. If Antonio couldn't do nothing else, he could slang some good ass dick.

"You can let yourself out now," I said, pulling the covers over my body.

"Damn, so I can't even spend the night? That's some fucked up shit, Trinity."

"Antonio, get the hell out. You came over here for one thing, and you got it. Now, you can leave. Ain't shit change. We're not together, and we're not gonna get back together. Bye, nigga."

He smacked his lips. "See, you didn't even think about it."

"There's nothing to think about! You constantly cheat on me, and you think I'm supposed to deal with that shit? No. I'm tired. I don't wanna go through that anymore. I got a funeral to go to in the morning. Now, if you could just leave, that would be great."

He was quiet for a moment, but eventually he got his ass outta my bed and started putting his clothes back on.

"Can't believe you're kicking me out," he muttered.

"Yeah, and I can't believe you were still cheating. I really shouldn't have let you into my damn apartment." I sat all the way up so I could look at him.

"Trinity, what do you want me to do? I'll do anything to—"

"You wanna know the most crazy part about all of this? You've never apologized to me. You've never cared enough to apologize. All you did was Come over here, dick me down, then act like nothing ever happened."

He rubbed the back of his head with that dumb ass look on his face. He didn't even have shit to say, because he knew what I said was true.

"I apologize when I be fuckin'." he said as I threw the covers off my legs.

"Nigga, no you don't. You always lying about some shit. Now get your lying ass up out my apartment," I stood on the other side of the bed watching and waiting for him to get the hell out.

"Am I gonna see you tomorrow?"

"Probably, but I'm going to the funeral to support Semaj. Don't be trying to talk to me during the service either, because I'll embarrass you in front of your family."

He looked like he wanted to say something, but instead, he just nodded, the proceeded to leave. I followed behind him and locked the door once he was gone.

I let out a loud sigh of relief. I should've just stayed at Semaj's place. At least that way, I wouldn't have had sex with his stupid ass.

"I've got to do better," I muttered as I walked back to my room.

My phone was vibrating on the dresser, so I quickly grabbed it, only to nervously sit it back down. Did I mention that I gave Tristan my number?

4

SEMAJ

Sleep didn't come easy for me last night. I couldn't stop thinking about my dad and how different things would've been if I actually talked to him. I thought about my mom, too. I just wish she would've never gotten addicted to drugs. I just wish I could've had a normal life.

I wasn't ready to see my dad's side of the family. I avoided them for a reason. I hated talking to any of them. I could barely tolerate Tristan.

Speaking of Tristan, he showed up extra early to my house this morning. He said he was here to make sure I actually got up and attended the funeral. Now, why wouldn't I want to say the last good-byes to my father?

I looked at myself in the mirror to make sure I was presentable. Eyes were red and low from the lack of sleep, my cream-colored pants suit was simple, but enough, and I had my hair in a low slick ponytail. I did my makeup, but that was to cover the bags and dark circles around my eyes. I didn't want to do this, but I knew I had to.

"This really what you're wearing?" Tristan asked as I made my way into the living room.

I looked down at my outfit. "Yes. Is something wrong with it?"

"It's a funeral, Semaj. Why can't you just be normal and wear black? You're gonna bring so much attention to yourself."

I shrugged. "Who cares what I have on? We're there to lay my dad to rest, not to worry about what the hell I'm wearing."

"Aight. You right, let's go."

I slowly followed him to his car and got in the passenger seat. It felt like my heart was in my throat, and that empty feeling was in my chest again.

"This will be over before I know it," I told myself.

"Man, you good? You about to start crying and shit?"

I shook my head. As much as I wanted to cry, I didn't. I already knew I wasn't going to cry at the funeral. I stopped crying years ago. I believe I was fifteen.

It was the first time I'd ever walked in on my mom doing drugs. Not only was she high out of her mind, but she was also letting some big, ugly, black man have sex with her limp body. Yeah, I knew my mom was doing drugs, but I'd never seen her like this.

I went in my room and cried like a baby. It was one of those loud, ugly cries too. But, that's when I realized crying solves nothing. I could've sat in my room and cried all night about my mom being a crackhead, but then what? After I was done crying, she'd still be a crackhead, right?

"I'm good," I let him know.

"You sure? I mean, you don't have to act tough today. You did just lose a parent."

"I said I'm okay, Tristan. I'm not going to cry. Are you? I'm just asking because I know your mom is gonna be there, and—"

"Fuck that bitch," he spat. "I don't have a mom. I got an egg donor, but that's about it." I couldn't even imagine how it would feel to have a mom that didn't want you. It was pretty sad.

"If it makes you feel any better, I don't like her either." I gave him a small smile.

He glanced at me and chuckled. "You don't like anyone, Semaj. I'm shocked you and Trinity are even still friends."

"Speaking of Trinity, could you not try to get with her please? I want my friends to stay as far away from you as possible. Plus, she's with Antonio. You know, your cousin?"

"She told me she wasn't with him. Plus, I don't give a fuck about that nigga." he said it so easily.

"Well, you should! You don't do stuff like that to family."

"You're the last person that needs to be talking about family, you don't even talk to us. Didn't even call to see how we're doing or anything. You don't give a fuck about us."

I fought the urge to roll my eyes at him. "Okay, well y'all don't call me either, so I guess we're even."

"Because no one wants to deal with your wannabe white ass." I snapped my head in his direction.

"I do not want to be white! Why do you keep saying shit like that?"

"You tried so hard to bury the hood in you, but I know that shit still in there. It's all good, though. It's gonna come out soon."

My face fell. "And what exactly do you mean by that? Why does it bother you so much that I don't let where I came from define me?"

"It doesn't bother me," he chuckled.

"Clearly it does. You always have something to say about it. So, I wanna know what the problem is."

"You fake, Semaj. You put on this white girl persona, acting like you were born in the suburbs. Acting like you ain't never had to fight for your life in the hood. Acting like you didn't use to struggle. You used to go days without eating. Them niggas ya moms used to bring over would try to rape you, right? You've seen plenty of dead bodies in your life—"

"Shut up, Tristan!" He was bringing up memories that I tried my hardest to burry.

"Why? That's you, right? That used to be your life. Your clothes used to always smell like piss. But, you got the nerve to turn your nose up at us. Not talking to your dad's side of the family like you don't fit right in with us. That shit annoying, bruh."

"Fuck you. It's my life. I can do whatever the hell I want with my life. Just because I don't act hood—"

"They're gonna try to kill you," He said with no emotion in his voice.

"Huh?" I asked, eyebrows coming together in confusion. "What are you talking about?"

"I wasn't gonna tell you. I was gonna let it surprise yo' uppity ass, but I can't. I'm not that type of nigga. You know how much money you sitting on right now?"

I shook my head. "No..."

"Well, the family does. They know, and believe me, they're mad. They're mad that you got everything. The houses, the cars, and the businesses. Them niggas never came around, but watch how many people about to be at this funeral. Fuckin' watch."

At this point, my heart was trying to beat out of my chest. I don't want any of this if people — my own family were going to try to kill me over.

"Well, I don't want it, then! This shit isn't worth losing my life over! Tell them that they can have it!"

"Nah," he shook his head. "Hell nah. You can't and won't give them shit. I got you, though. Ain't nobody gonna touch you as long as I'm around." He was confident with his answer, but it didn't make me feel better.

"So, that's why you asked if I owned a gun?" I asked, quietly.

"Yeah. Shit about to get real for you. Nigga's gon' try to steal your empire. That's why they killed your dad. He was making too much money and killing the game. They couldn't handle it."

"Empire? Tristan, what the hell are you talking about?"

"So, you really didn't know? You didn't know who your pops was in the streets?"

Clearly, I didn't! I didn't know anything about the streets! I worked my ass off, so I wouldn't ever have to be in the streets again.

"No, I didn't." I said, flipping my ponytail off my shoulder.

"He ran Atlanta," he let me know. "All the drugs coming through here? That shit was your pops. Nigga done seen more money than you'll ever imagine."

"So... he sold drugs? He was a drug dealer?"

"He was more than a drug dealer. Think of it as a distributor. The family knows that. Shit, your mom knew that. Where the hell you think she was getting her drugs from? You ever wonder how your parents met?"

I opened my mouth to say something, but nothing came out. My mom was buying drugs from my daddy? He knew she was a crackhead, but he didn't care.

Why didn't he try to get her help? Why didn't he just stop giving it to her? Did he know what I was going through, and just not care? My childhood was terrible because of him! I know this sounds bad, but I didn't feel as bad as I did about his death anymore. He was the reason my mom was gone.

"Wow," I finally said after a while. "My dad killed my mom."

"Nah," he said. "Your dad didn't force her to do that shit. It was—"

"Shut the fuck up, Tristan! He killed my mom! He clearly didn't give a fuck about me because he would've been telling her to stop doing drugs, not giving them to her!" I was furious.

The real reason my dad left everything to me was because he knew. He knew what the fuck he did. That was the real reason he didn't come around. He knew he wouldn't be able to look me in the face knowing he was the reason my mom was on drugs. He didn't even come to her funeral.

"I feel like I'm about to fucking puke," I said, rolling down my window to let in fresh air.

"What? Man, hell nah. Don't fucking throw up in my shit, Semaj."

We pulled up to the church and I could already tell it was packed. I'd never seen any of the people who were standing in the parking lot.

"You know them?" I asked, watching him reach in the glove compartment and pull a gun out.

"Hell nah. Most of them are here to be nosey, and the rest of them are here to kill you." He kept saying things like that like it wasn't a big deal.

"What?! I don't wanna go in there!"

"I gotchu, Semaj. Come on." He got out the car and I watched him come to my side of the car. I didn't wanna get out. My stomach was turning, and I felt like I was going to pass out. I didn't wanna lose my life over my dad.

Tristan opened my door and I looked up at him. "Come on, Semaj. You don't have anything to worry about."

But I did.

"I'm scared," I let him know. Just as I said it, Antonio made his way toward us.

"What's up, nigga?" he asked, dapping Tristan up. "You know any of these mothafuckas?"

Tristan shook his head. "Man, hell nah. Ain't nobody looking familiar to me."

"You strapped?" Antonio glanced at me when he said it.

"Always, bruh."

"Hey, Semaj." Antonio said, with a sympathetic look on his face. "How you feeling? It's fucked up how they killed—"

"I'm fine, Antonio. Thank you." I stepped out of the car and smoothed my outfit down. I let Tristan lead the way as I followed behind him. Antonio was walking next to me, and right now, I was wishing I was anywhere but here.

As we stepped into the church, I could hear people crying. All eyes were on us as we made our way to the front. There wasn't anywhere to sit, but from the look that was on Tristan's face, I could tell he was gonna make someone move.

"Ayo, get the hell up," Tristan said to some women I'd never seen before. They instantly twisted their faces up.

"No. We were here first. Should've got her earlier," she snapped.

"Bitch, get the fuck up before I blast yo' dumb ass. Who the fuck are you, anyway?" Tristan was drawing even more attention to us, and my entire body began to get hot.

"I'm Dwayne's girlfriend!" she yelled way louder than she needed to.

Girlfriend? Didn't he have a wife, though?

Tristan laughed, then forcefully pulled her up by her arm. She let out a small shriek as she fell to the floor.

"Sit down, Semaj." Tristan demanded. I watched the girl pull herself up off the floor. "All y'all can get the fuck up too, unless you want the same shit to happen to you."

The other two women quickly got up and we gladly took their seats. That's when I finally looked up and saw my daddy's lifeless body lying in the casket.

I didn't know how to feel. I could feel people staring at me, but I knew half of them were family. Tristan's mom was sitting directly behind us, and I could hear her talking shit under her breath.

"Can't believe he left everything to this ungrateful bitch," she muttered. "Little hoe doesn't even claim us." I wanted to turn around, and say something to her, but I decided against it. She wasn't worth it.

"You got the nerve to talk about someone not claiming family when you're a whole dead-beat ass mother," Tristan snapped as he turned to look at her. She ignored him, though. She kept sitting there like she didn't say a thing to her. "Stupid ass bitch," he spat, turning back around.

"Excuse me," I heard Trinity's voice from behind me. "I need to sit right here." I turned to look at her. She was making her way down the row of people, ignoring all the dirty looks she was getting.

I was so glad she was here. Words couldn't even explain how much I needed her here. She plopped down right next to Renee, Tristan's mom.

"Hey," she smiled at me. "I didn't expect this many people to be here."

I nodded. "Me either."

"Wassup, shawty?" Tristan asked, looking at her. She gave him a small wave as she shyly looked away from him.

What the hell was that? I eyed Tristan, but he ignored me.

"I would like to start this off by saying Dwayne was a good man," a light skinned woman said, standing at the podium. "He was a great husband, father, and provider."

"Great father?" I scoffed. She was only saying that because it sounded good. How was he a great father, and I didn't even know he had a wife? He was a great father, but he killed my mom? This woman didn't know what the hell she was talking about.

"His death came so suddenly. I wasn't expecting to be a widow at age twenty-six. I didn't know—"

"Bitch, you ain't the only one he gave a ring to!" someone erupted from the crowd. "He even told me that y'all weren't even married! He knew you were the only with him for his money!"

"Oh shit," Tristan muttered. "Ain't no good gonna come to this."

The dark-skinned woman emerged from the crowd of people and marched straight to the wife.

"Not really married? Bitch, I got his whole last name! You think you're somebody because he gave you a promise ring?"

"Promise ring?! Bitch, I'll beat yo' ass in front of all these people!"

Was this really happening right now? Were they really about to fight at a funeral?

"Let's go then, bitch! You're just mad because you're not really married!"

The dark-skinned woman didn't even wait for the wife to reply before she delivered a punch directly in her mouth. Once that first punch was thrown, chaos exploded. There were people trying to break up the fight, and there were also people trying to join in on the fight. Random people were fighting, and I was wondering why all this was happening right now.

"What the hell?" I asked, looking around. "Tristan why—" My sentence was cut short by a punch sent to the back of my head.

"I've been waiting for this shit, bitch. I couldn't stand your ass when you first came outta your crack headed ass mama's pussy!" Renee said as I stood up.

See, I wasn't no damn fighter. I tried to avoid confrontation as much as I could. Just because I wasn't a fighter, that didn't mean that I couldn't fight.

"Don't talk about my mama, bitch!" I hollered, as I pulled her by her hair. Once I had that bitch over the seat, I started delivering punches like I was trying to kill her.

"Whoa, whoa, whoa!" Tristan yelled. "Yo, what the fuck?!" I knew he was yelling at me to get off his mama, but she started it. She shouldn't have put her hands on me to begin with.

We fell to the ground, and I wrestled my way on top of her. I tried pressing my thumbs in her eyes because I was trying to pop them bitches out. She bit me like I was a fucking animal, and that only fueled my anger. Before I could even react, my ponytail was being pulled in another direction, and even more blows were coming at me. I had no idea who was fighting me now, but I was trying my hardest to get away from them.

"Let me go!" I screamed, trying to shield my face from the hits it was receiving. Right after I yelled that, I felt another set of hands start hitting me too.

I was kicking and screaming but nothing was stopping them. I could hear Trinity calling my name, but I couldn't open my eyes to look at her. From the sounds of it, she was fighting too.

POP! POP! POP!

Gunshots rang out, causing everyone around me to duck in cover.

"Oh my God," I said, finally able to look around. It looked like everyone in the Church was fighting, running, or screaming. I could hear kids crying out for their mama's, people yelling for help, and people cussing, trying to get to a safe place.

"Semaj!" Tristan yelled. "Let's go!" he helped me up off the floor and we took off running towards the back of the church.

"What the hell is going on?" I asked, out of breath. "Why are they shooting?"

"Most likely, they were aiming at you. Hurry up and get in the car. Someone is probably following us."

I let out a small sigh of relief when we finally made it outside. Antonio and Trinity were already out there waiting for us.

"Look at your fuckin' face, bitch." Trinity said as she examined me. I didn't bother responding. I figured my face was messed up after those bitches jumped me.

"Come on! What the hell y'all just standing there for?" Antonio yelled. He was right. We were just standing there like there wasn't just people shooting at me.

We took off running towards the car that Tristan was already in. It felt like my chest was going to cave in. It'd been so long since I ran.

"What the fuck?!" I yelled once we were all safely in the car. My nose was bleeding, lip was busted, and it felt like someone tried to claw my face off.

"That was some ghetto ass shit," Trinity said. "Who starts fucking shooting at a damn funeral? Like, what the fuck were they even shooting at?"

"Semaj. Half the people in there wants her dead." Tristan let her know. Every time he said it, my heart sank. I didn't do anything to anyone but now, all of a sudden, they want me dead?

"What? Why? Semaj, what the hell you do to your dad's side of the family?" she asked, looking at me.

"I didn't do anything. They're mad because my daddy left everything to me. They need to be mad at him, not me." I folded my arms and shook my head. This was some of the dumbest shit.

"It's only gonna get worse from here, Semaj. You need to prepare yourself." Antonio said.

"Why? Why can't I tell them I don't want it? This isn't fair!" I was damn near pouting like a three-year-old, but that's how I felt. They didn't even talk to me about it to see if I really wanted this or not.

"Tell them you don't want it? You didn't tell her, did you?" Antonio looked at Tristan and Tristan gave a light shrug.

"I mean, a little bit. I touched on the subject."

"Tell me what?"

"You're gonna be the one that runs Atlanta now. Dwayne's dead, so that shit gets passed down to you."

Wait. What?

"Huh? So, I'm a drug dealer, now?" I asked, feeling my heart rate sped up.

"It's so much more to it, Semaj." Antonio let me know. "So much more."

5

TRAP

"Bitches dumb as fuck," my younger brother Two laughed as he walked beside me, into the gas station. "I'm telling them all the same shit and they all believe it. This shit too easy,"

"Until you come across a crazy bitch that burns your house down while you're sleeping in it at night," I laughed. "Yeah, lemme get twenty on pump two." I said, sliding the cashier a twenty.

"Nah. Ain't none of them bold enough to do some dumb shit like that."

"That's what you think, nigga. You gon' learn the hard way. Watch."

We got back to the car, and I peeped a white Cadillac sitting across the street watching us. I'd spotted that shit when we first pulled up, but I thought I was trippin'. But, now that I was looking at them niggas again, they were definitely watching us.

Two was still running his mouth about bitches, but I was tuning his dumb ass out. Something wasn't sitting right with this shit. I watched closely as the tinted window slowly rolled down.

"Shit," I hissed, quickly getting in the car.

"What's going on?" Two asked, watching me start the car. "Did you even pump that gas, nigga?" I ignored him as I sped out the gas station.

That's when bullets start flying.

"Oh hell nah!" Two said, immediately pulling his strap out. I kept speeding as the Cadillac started to follow us. "The fuck is that?!"

"Eastside niggas," I let him know. "I saw them when we first pulled up."

"Why the hell you didn't say shit? You know my trigger finger been itching, lately." I ignored Two as I focused on the road. I knew Two was gonna start blasting at these niggas at any moment. "Fuck you running for, Trap? Let's give these niggas what they fuckin' want!"

"Get them off my ass, nigga! Fuck you doing all that talking for?"

Two gave me a small smile before rolling his window down, then popping out of it, aiming his gun directly at their car. Two lived for shit like this. Nigga would catch bodies like it was a fucking sport. That nigga didn't have cognitions. He could kill somebody's son or daughter and not give one fuck about that shit.

He shot one of their tires out, and I watched them swerve in the rearview mirror. I took a sharp right turn, accidentally driving through somebody's yard, but I didn't give a fuck. Them niggas were still right behind us.

"Two, what the fuck you doing, nigga?! Kill them niggas! Get the fuckin' driver!" I yelled.

"Aight man, shut the hell up!" He aimed his gun out the window again and pulled the trigger. This time, get got the driver right in the head and their car start swerving out of control.

"Yeah. That's what the fuck I'm talking about." I said, as Two pulled himself back in the car.

"Bitch ass niggas. They picked the wrong mothafuckas to mess with today," he said as he dropped his gun on the floor behind him. "Can't believe that shit."

"I wasted twenty dollars," I muttered. "I should go back there and make them niggas pay me."

"Nigga, you ain't strapped? Why didn't you blast them fools when you first saw them? The hell you on, bruh?"

"I'm not trigger happy like you, nigga. That shit could've went all the way left. Innocent people could've lost their lives."

He smacked his lips. "Man, fuck them. They shouldn't have been in the way then. Shit."

I ignored him as I kept driving. I went back to my side of town to get gas, then pulled up in Burger King's parking lot.

"You hungry? I ain't ate shit all day," I said, finding a park.

"You already know if you're paying, I'm eating, nigga. I don't even know what the hell you asked for." He rubbed his hands together as I got out the car.

"Who the fuck said I was paying? I just asked if you were hungry." I chuckled.

"Oh shit, Dwayne's funeral got shot up today." he laughed, looking down at his phone. "That shit fucked up."

"Damn. I expected that shit to happen, though. Shit doesn't even surprise me. Anybody die?"

He shrugged as I opened the door. "I don't know. Some bitch made a status about it. Glad I ain't go to that shit. I would've started shooting back, making mothafuckas know how the fuck I'm coming." he nodded.

"Trinity, I really don't even care what you have to say to me right now. With the news I just found out, and my daddy's funeral getting shot up? The only thing I wanna do is go home and go to sleep. I want to forget this day ever happened." The girl standing in line in front of us said on the phone.

She talked so proper. Sounded like she knew what she wanted out of life. I let my eyes roam all over her body in the grey leggings she was wearing. She wasn't wearing any draws. I could tell.

"No! I'm not going out tonight, Trinity! Why do you keep asking? My answer is going to remain the same. No. Nope. I don't wanna shake my butt on anyone. I told you what I was doing tonight. End of discussion."

"Damn, nigga," Two said, making me look at him. "Put your tongue back in your mouth."

She turned around to look at us, and I quickly averted my eyes from her ass to her eyes. She had a scratch under one eye, and a busted lip. Immediately, I was turned off. I couldn't fuck with a bitch who thought it was okay to let her nigga beat on her and shit.

"You two can go in front of me," she said politely. "I'm not sure what I want yet."

"Shit, say less. I'm hungry as fuc—"

"Nah, ma, you good. We know how to be patient." I let her know.

She looked at me like she wanted to say something, but she decided against it. She turned back around and finished having her conversation.

"What's going on with you today? What you being extra nice for? She ain't gon' give you the pussy. You know you don't get along with boujiee bitches," Two laughed, causing shawty to turn around and look at us again.

"Excuse me?" she asked, with her face twisting up. I sighed to myself. Two was always doing shit like this. When he found someone he thought was attractive? He would talk shit to get their attention like a little ass boy. "Could you not—"

"Nobody was talking to you, shawty," he cut in. "Turn yo' ass around and finish minding your business."

"Mind my business? You were talking about me. That is my business!"

Shawty looked good as fuck. Yeah, I could tell she tried too hard to act white, but that shit didn't take from her beauty. Her ass was the perfect size. I could have hella fun throwing her ass around.

"You don't know that. I could've been talking about the woman standing in front of you. You one of those bitches that think they know everything, huh?"

She stared at Two for a while before she just decided to turn around and ignore him. She should've done that in the first place. Two will argue with anyone about anything. That's just the type of nigga he was.

"Girl, I don't know who the hell that was. I'm standing here minding my business and he's behind me calling me out my name and stuff. I need to get away from this side of town ASAP. I can't believe I'm even over here." she said into the phone.

"Yo, ain't nobody call you a bitch. You over there lying on me and shit?" Two was laughing because shawty was feeding into his childish ass games. They'd be fucking by the end of the week. That's usually how it went.

"Why are you still talking to me? I'm over here minding my business—"

"Nah, you over there looking like you just got your ass beat. Probably because of that mouth—"

"Fuck this," she spat, starting to make her way towards the door. "I can't stand black men! Y'all are so childish! I'm about to start dealing with women because I cannot!" She stormed out of Burger King without even getting anything to eat.

"Damn," Two chuckled. "Bitch was mad as hell."

"She sounded like she was having a bad day and you just came and made it worse."

"What? The hell makes you think she had a bad day? You swear you be knowing people."

"Nah, never said I knew her, but when we walked up she was talking about how her daddy's funeral got shot up and shit."

"Word? You stay listening to somebody's conversation. That's why I hate talking on the phone around yo' nosey ass."

"Fuck you," I snickered. "You always talking extra loud anyway. But nah, you think her pops was Dwayne, though? Didn't his shit get shot up today, too?"

"Nah," he said, shaking his head. "Dwayne had a son. I think his name was Semaj or some shit. Don't you have a file on that nigga's life?"

"Yeah, but I don't remember seeing anything about a son. I might've read it, and just forgot. A nigga like me smokes too damn much."

So, after we got our food and shit, we pulled up to Two's crib to chill and shit. He kept talking about how he'd met some bitch the other day and she was supposed to be on her way over there to chill.

"She says she has a cute ass friend, so I told her to bring her so you won't be feeling like a third wheel and shit." he said as I broke down some weed on his coffee table.

"Man, hell nah. I always get stuck with the ugly bitches. The friends ain't never cute."

"That last bitch was cute. Her hair was just a little fucked up, but—"

"Nah, nigga. She had more hair on her pussy than I got on my head. She was tryna tell me she wasn't that hairy when I was looking right at the shit. Bitch had the nerve to tell me that real men don't let a little hair bother them. The fuck?"

"Damn," he laughed. "I didn't know shawty was like that. I can't stand a bitch that acts like she's afraid to shave. Shit nasty."

"Then, the bitch before that? Man, she smelled like a fish market. I'm done taking one for the team. Your bitch that's coming over can bring her friend, but I'm not showing no damn interest. Fuck that."

He nodded. "I feel you, nigga. Maybe this one will be different, though. You might actually like her."

"Don't give a fuck. I'm acting like shawty ain't even there. I'm not gonna get her hopes up or nothing."

Just as I said that, the doorbell rang. Those bitches wasted no time coming over here. I let out a small sigh as Two got up to open the door.

Moments later, a pretty ass dark skinned chick made her way into the living room with nothing but smiles on her face.

"Trap, this is Trinity. Trinity, this is my older brother Trap." Two introduced us.

"Hey," she said, sitting on the couch that Two was just sitting on.

"Oh," Two said again. "And this is her friend..."

"Semaj," the other girl snapped, sitting as far as she could from me on the couch. "Can't even believe I'm here," she muttered, pulling out her phone.

I looked at her, finally realizing she was the same girl from Burger King earlier. I wasn't sure if Two noticed that shit or if he just didn't care. It was pretty hard to get that nigga to care about something.

"Y'all got anything to drink?" Trinity asked.

"Hell yeah. You tryna get drunk, or you just want some juice or something?" Two stood up, waiting for her answer.

"Shit, both. It's never a bad time to drink," He nodded and made his way into the kitchen, and I turned my attention back to Semaj.

She had changed since I'd saw her at Burger King. She had on some tight ass pants, and some white blouse looking shit. I didn't know what the fuck it was about shawty, but I was drawn to her ass.

"You just gon' sit over there not saying shit the whole time?" I asked, watching her look up from her phone to look at me. She let her eyes roam all over my body before she twisted her face up a little.

"That was the plan. I'm only here because I was basically forced. I just don't understand why I had to come over here because she had a dick appointment."

I glanced at Trinity who shrugged like she didn't care. "I told you, you could leave after I got here, but you decided to come all the way in here."

"What happened to ya face? Ya man ain't do that shit did he?" I questioned, because the shit was bothering me. I just needed to know if a nigga did that shit to her or not.

"Well," she said, flipping her ponytail off her shoulder. "Today, I went to my dad's funeral, and got jumped." She gave me a sarcastic smile and I laughed. I tried to hold that shit in, but it didn't work.

"What? Why you get jumped?"

"Because my dad's side of the family never liked me. Then on top of that, he died, and left everything in his Will to me, so they're mad. After they jumped me, people started shooting. It was so embarrassing."

Two came back in the living room with a cup for Trinity, then sat down next to her.

"Damn, that's fucked up. Who the hell was shooting at your daddy's funeral?" I finished rolling the blunt and watched her text away on her phone.

"I'm not sure. I didn't stay to find out, either."

I nodded. At least she wasn't stupid. "Aye, your pops name Dwayne?"

She looked up at me with a lifted eyebrow. "Yeah. Why? You know him?"

"Hell nah," I lied.

Hell yeah, I knew him. I was the one who killed that nigga.

6

SEMAJ

I didn't even know why I agreed to come over here with Trinity. I always got stuck with the ugly guys. Trap? He really let people call him that? But, his brother's name wasn't any better. Either way, I was ready to get the hell out of here.

Trap was ugly... Well, I wasn't even sure if that was the word to describe him. He was more scary-looking than he was ugly. He had hair, that stopped right at his shoulders, his skin was light, beard was long and full, and he had tattoos on his face. Actually, from the looks of it, Trap had tattoos on every inch of his body. Even down to his fingers.

"So, your real name is Trap?" I asked, after Two and Trinity disappeared to a different room. I knew once Trinity started drinking she was going to be ready to get nasty. I should've went home, but I really didn't feel comfortable knowing that there would be two men here and she was by herself.

"Nah," he laughed as I watched him lick the blunt. He already had one rolled, but now he was rolling another one? "That's just what niggas call me."

"So, what's your real name?"

He looked at me, while raising an amused brow. "Why? You the feds or some shit?"

I rolled my eyes. "Umm, no. I would just rather call you by your real name. Trap sounds… hood."

He let out a loud laugh like I had just told the funniest joke. "You funny. Anybody ever tell you that?"

I shrugged. "I mean, I've heard it before."

"Mega. My real name is Mega."

"Oh," I giggled. "That's kinda cute. I'd rather call you Mega than Trap. It sounds so much better." I nodded.

"Word? So, I can call you Semmy?"

"What? No. My name is Semaj. That's what you can call me."

"Nah, I'ma call you Semmy. That shit sound good." He smiled as I shook my head.

"Well, I'm not going to answer to that." I felt my phone vibrate in my hand and I looked down at it. Marcus was back in town and wanted to see me. I still was a little mad at him for making me walk home, so I really wasn't in the mood to see him.

"I'm not going to answer to that," he mocked. "You proper as fuck."

"Proper? No, I just have a high school education. Is your brother's real name Two? Like, the number two or…"

"Nah, his name Maurice. He was born right after me, so our mom started calling him Two. I guess that shit just stuck." he let me know.

Two was very unattractive too. He didn't have the tattoos on his face like his brother, but he had them everywhere else. They covered his neck, letting me know that he was crazy. Any man with tattoos all on his neck was crazy. It was a fact. He was about the same height as Mega, skin was a little lighter, and he also didn't have any hair. He kept his hair cut low.

There was something eerie about Two, though. He gave me a weird vibe in the short amount of time that I'd known him. I kind of had the same feeling about Mega, but that was only because he said something about my dad. I just thought it was a little weird that he asked about my dad. He knew my dad's first name and everything, but then says he doesn't know him?

Something just wasn't sitting right with me, but it could've been because I knew people were trying to kill me now. It also could've just been me and my bad nerves. I did get shot at today.

My phone began to ring in my hand, and I glanced down at it. For some reason, my heart sank when I saw Tristan's name pop up on the screen.

"Hello?" I answered, hesitantly.

"Aye, where you at? You good?" he asked.

"Yes, I'm fine. I'm just hanging out with a... friend." I glanced in Mega's direction who was now lighting his blunt.

"Cool. I need you to swing by. We got some shit we need to take care of." I didn't like the way that sounded. Plus, being around Tristan was a constant reminder about how my life had suddenly taken a drastic turn for the worse.

"Right now? Tristan, I'm kinda busy. It can't wait until tomorrow?"

"I mean yeah we can wait, but you might be dead by then." he let out a small chuckle, and I wanted to just scream at the top of my lungs.

"What? Why would I—"

"Semaj, just come through, man. I wouldn't be calling you if it wasn't important."

"Fine," I sighed. "I'll be over there soon." I ended the call, not even waiting for him to respond.

"That was your man calling?" Mega asked as I looked up at him.

"No. That was my cousin. I don't have a game because men play games."

"We be playing games?" he wondered. "Nah, shawty. You just be fucking with the wrong niggas. Once you fuck with a real nigga, you not gonna be saying that shit." He licked his lips, then passed the blunt that I politely declined.

"I don't smoke," I let him know.

"Yet," he muttered.

I ignored him as I stood to my feet. "Well, Mega," I started, flipping my ponytail. "It was nice to meet you. Maybe one day, we can hang out again." I was lying, but he didn't need to know that. I didn't plan on seeing Mega ever again after today.

"True shit," he said, standing up too. He towered over me and smelled good as hell. I almost didn't want him to get out of my personal area just so I could keep smelling him. "Lemme get your number. When you're not too busy, we can chill by ourselves and shit."

My mouth went dry. I wasn't expecting him to say anything like that. I didn't think he'd even want to see me again after this.

"Um... sure," I said, slowly taking his phone from his hand and storing my number in it.

After that, he walked me outside to my car. I still felt a little wrong for leaving Trinity here by herself, but I was hoping and praying they weren't plotting on her.

"Oh damn. This you?" he questioned, looking at my car.

I smiled to myself. "Yep."

My 20116 all black BMW was my baby. I saved all of my money until I could afford it. This was one of my biggest accomplishments.

We finally said our last goodbyes, then I got in my car and pulled off. He watched me drive away until we couldn't see each other anymore. He was nicer than I expected him to be, but that didn't change the fact that he wasn't my type.

I wasn't into guys like him. Tattoos turned me off. I didn't like hair on men unless it was a curly fro, or dreads. His made him look a little scary. I didn't ask him where he worked at, but I was almost sure it was doing something illegal.

"He wasn't even cute," I muttered as I drove. Every time I tried to get my mind off of him, I would just end up thinking about him all over again. I didn't know what that was, but it was bothering me. I didn't even do things like this over Marcus. The man I once thought I wanted to be with.

It took me about twenty minutes, but I finally pulled up to Tristan's house, and he was standing outside, smoking. The few years he'd been living here, I'd never come over. I just didn't see a point to. We barely talked anyway.

"What's up? You didn't run into anybody did you?" he asked, blowing smoke from his mouth. I twisted my face up.

"Umm, no. Who was I supposed to run into?"

He shrugged. "Shit, I don't know. Ain't no telling who's all lurking, waiting to catch yo' ass off guard."

I sighed loudly. "So, what am I supposed to do? What if they do catch me off guard? I'm just supposed to let them kill me? Do I run? What if I'm getting shot at? Then what?"

"Chill, nigga. That's what the hell I called you over here for. Come on." He turned to walk into his house and I followed close behind him. With the way he was just talking, he had me afraid to do anything by myself. Now, I felt like someone was going to always be following me until they finally killed me like they wanted to.

"I don't want to live like this. I can't just move out of the state? Will they leave me alone then?"

"Nah," he said, shaking his head. "It ain't that easy." He closed and locked the door behind me as I took in the appearance of his house.

It was nice. A large flat screen TV was mounted on the wall, his couches were black and leather, and there was a small glass table sitting in the middle of the living room floor. He didn't have the walls painted, and he also didn't have any pictures hanging up. I could definitely tell the house was decorated by a man.

"Nice little place you got here," I let him know as I sat down on the couch.

He ignored my compliment as he came to stand in front of me.

"Here," he said, shoving a gun in my face. "Show me how to take the safety off."

I looked at the gun for a moment before I looked back up at him. I didn't know the first thing about guns. All I knew is they killed people.

"I don't even know what that is. Tristan."

He nodded, then sat down next to me. For hours, we talked about guns. Well, it was mostly him talking, explaining everything that I needed to know, and me asking questions ever so often. Guns scared

me. I'd never even held one before because I didn't want to accidentally shoot myself or something.

"Aight, we'll get to the big guns later," he let me know. "You need to
know how to shoot this bitch,"

My heart wanted to jump out my chest. He wanted me to shoot it?
There wasn't anything else I could do to protect myself? I couldn't just
go to the police and let them know that people were out there trying
to kill me?

"I don't think—"

"Nah, don't even start that shit. You can't be acting scared. Being
scared causes you to fuck up. We don't need that shit happening.
Tomorrow, we're going to the shooting range."

"But, what if I don't want to?"

He shrugged. "Then, we can start planning your funeral now. It's
really up to you."

I sighed to myself. This wasn't the life I wanted. I didn't wanna live
in fear. Shit, I really didn't even wanna be seen with Tristan or anyone
else from my dad's side of the family, but I guess this was the way
things had to be now.

"Fine. I'll go." I said in defeat.

"Yeah, I know—"

BOOM!

My hand went to my chest as I looked at Tristan with wide eyes. It
sounded like someone was trying to blow his house up.

"Yo, hell nah, man." He shot up from the couch and went to open
the front door. I was afraid, but I got up and stood behind him.

"What happened?" I whispered.

"We gotta go."

"Huh? For what? Why—" My words got caught in my throat once I
let my eyes land on what he was looking at.

My car. My BMW that I worked so hard to pay for was up in
flames. I could feel my heart pounding, but I could barely breathe.
Fear and sadness clawed through me, as my stomach knotted.

What?" was all I was able to say after a while. "Why?"

"Come on, Semaj." Tristan demanded as he slammed his door shut, then locked it. "We gotta go. Now." He grabbed me by the arm, then lead me into the living room where he grabbed my purse and his gun, then we went into the kitchen. I was still in shock. My car was gone, just like that.

Tristan opened the door that led to the garage where his car was waiting on us. He seemed like he was in a hurry, but my legs could barely move.

"Let's go, Semaj! Why you walking like you got all day?" I could hear the annoyance in her voice, but I didn't care. He didn't know what the hell I was going through. My heart felt like it had just been kicked out of my chest, then stepped on.

"My car," I said quietly once I slid into the passenger seat. "They really destroyed my car."

"I know, Semaj. Them niggas know where the fuck you are. We need to get the fuck up outta here."

"But how? How do they—"

"Because they followed you. They probably been following your ass all day without you even realizing it." He started the car, then let his garage up. I swear, I felt my heart stop when I saw someone standing there waiting for us.

I opened my mouth to scream, but nothing came out. That's when Tristan put the car in reverse and backed out as fast as he could. I thought the person standing there would jump out the way, but they didn't. Tristan ran them over like it was nothing.

"Goodness," I gasped, with a hand covering my mouth. The gunshots that came right after that could've given me a heart attack. I was screaming at the top of my lungs as Tristan sped off.

"Fuck," he muttered, looking in the rearview mirror. "These niggas ain't playing."

"All this over money?!" I yelled. I could feel the tears building up, but I refused to let them fall.

"Money and power will make niggas do crazy things, Semaj. You didn't learn that shit growing up?"

I shook my head. "No! I didn't hang out with people like y'all! I hung out with people who knew how to act! People who were classy! People who—"

"Yeah, Semaj I know! You hung out with white people! You hung out with them mothafuckas and started studying their every move! You hung out with them wishing you would've been born like that. Wishing you would've been born into money... Well, look nigga. You were! You were born into money, and now it's about to get yo' ass killed! You can take the person out the hood, but you can't take the hood out the person!"

"I'm not hood! I've never been hood! Even when I was living in those nasty, roach infested apartments, I still didn't act like y'all!"

He laughed bitterly. "Yes, you did. You used to steal honey buns out the corner store with us. You used to play outside with no fucking shoes on because you only had one pair and didn't wanna mess them up worse than they already were. You used to stay outside all day because you knew the power was off at your spot. Stop acting like we didn't come from the same place. Stop acting like—"

"Take me home, Tristan." I said calmly.

"Hell no. That's probably the first place they're gonna go. They waiting for you there."

I shook my head. "They probably don't even know where I live at. Take me home. I need to get a few things, anyway." I really just didn't want to be in the car with him anymore.

Tristan always wanted to bring up my past. He always wanted to remind me of things that I tried to forget on purpose. Things that make me cringe when I thought about it. There were things that happened to me that I didn't tell anyone. I refused to let anyone know about the things I went through. I felt like if I forgot it, that would be enough.

"Semaj," Tristan said, pulling an aggravated hand down his face. "You really don't need to go—"

"Tristan, I said take me home!" My blood was boiling with rage. The more I was around Tristan, the angrier I got. I was wishing he never even came to my place the other day. I just wish he would've left me alone.

The fifteen-minute ride to my place was a quiet one. He didn't even turn on the radio. I sat with my arms folded, staring out the window. My face was tight, and my body was stiff. I couldn't believe any of this was happening to me right now.

I saw the flashing lights of fire trucks as we got closer and closer to my house. I didn't think anything of it until we pulled up right in front of my place and I saw it up in flames.

"No!" I yelled, quickly unbuckling my seat belt and jumping out the car. Before I could step foot on the grass, I was being snatched up.

"I fucking told you, Semaj! Let's go!" Tristan yelled.

That was it for me. The tears were falling faster than I could catch them. I fought and screamed the entire time Tristan drug me back to the car.

At this point, I didn't care anymore. They had destroyed my car, and now my house. Everything I'd worked so hard for was gone. I didn't know where Tristan was taking me, but I was hoping he would turn on me, too, then kill me. I didn't have anything worth living for, anyway.

7

TRINITY

Two had given me life changing dick. He had put me in so many positions. I felt like we were doing yoga up in that bitch. Then on top of that? The nigga didn't get tired. I swear, it felt like we had sex for eight whole hours. My entire body was sore. It took me a little minute, but I was finally able to get up from his bed, then take my ass home. I had spent the night without even meaning to.

When I was leaving, Trap was laying on the couch with his eyes closed, making me think his ass was sleeping. Nigga scared the fuck outta me when he started talking.

"Tell Semmy to be expecting a call from me later," he said as I looked down at him.

"Who, nigga?"

"Your friend that you came with yesterday."

"Oh," I laughed, running my hands through my messy hair. "Semaj. Her name is—"

"I know what the fuck her name is. Just do what I said, aight?"

I twisted my face up. Who the hell did this nigga think he was talking to?

Two came out the bedroom in some sweats and no shirt on. Nigga was fine as hell. If he hadn't tried to kill my vagina last night, I probably would've been ready to jump his bones again right now.

"Damn," Two said, looking at me through tired eyes. "You were just gonna leave without saying shit to me? I don't get no goodbye kiss or nothing? You just out?"

"Boy," I giggled. "You didn't even want me to kiss you yesterday after you ate my boot—"

"Ayo," Trap snapped, now opening his eyes. "Y'all can't take this conversation somewhere else? A nigga over here tryna sleep."

"Nigga, you in my shit. You should've took yo' ass home if you didn't wanna be woken up outta your sleep and shit. Fuck outta here." Two turned his attention back to me and gave me a sexy ass smile. "But like I was saying, shawty. That's fucked up how you wasn't gonna say shit to me before you left."

"You looked like you were sleeping so peacefully. I didn't wanna—"

"Nah, fuck all that. You were tryna sneak up outta here. You got yo' man waiting for you at home or something?"

I shook my head. "What? Hell no. I don't even have a man. I was just ready to get home and shower. It had nothing to do with you." I was telling the truth. I really just wanted to be at my own place, in my own shower.

"Hell yeah, you were ready to leave," Trap said, sitting up on the couch. "How the hell were you gonna get home if Semmy took the car yesterday?"

My shoulders fell. Semaj damn sure did leave with her car. That shit had totally slipped my mind. I didn't know what the hell I was thinking.

"Shit," I muttered. I looked down at the floor before letting my eyes land on Two. "Can you take me home, please?"

He licked his lips, before he smiled at me. "Yeah, bring yo' ass."

He didn't bother to put a shirt on. Shit, honestly, I didn't think he even had on underwear either, because I could see his dick print perfectly.

I met Two at the gas station a few days ago. I saw him standing at his car pumping gas when I first pulled up. He saw me get out my car, then followed me all the way into the store like he didn't have anything better to do. He didn't approach me or anything. He just stood over there eyeing me like he was undressing me with his eyes.

I finally got tired of him staring at me like he didn't have any sense, so I turned to him and asked,

"You tryna pay my bills? You staring at me like you wanna pay them."

His fine ass licked his lips, pulled a tatted hand down his face, then said,

"Hell yeah." That shit caught me off guard, so, I gave him my number. Who would've known he would have devil dick?

"So, you gonna tell me where you live at, or you gonna keep daydreaming over there?" he asked, once we were in his car.

I told him my address, thinking he was going to put it in his GPS, but he didn't. He just started driving like he knew exactly where I lived.

He turned up the radio as loud as it would go, blaring some trap music that I'd never heard before. Hood niggas always play hood nigga music. While he rapped along and bobbed his head to the music, I looked down at my phone. I didn't have any texts or calls from Semaj, and that was weird.

"Could you turn the music down, please?" I damn near yelled over the music.

He quickly glanced at me before he turned the radio off completely. Nigga was extra. All he had to do was turn it down a little bit.

Swiping my finger across the screen, I clicked on Semaj's contact, then put the phone to my ear.

"You not calling your boyfriend, are you?" Two asked as I listened to the phone rang. "You need to go on and tell that nigga you found somebody else."

I snapped my head in his direction as the phone went to voicemail. That was weird because Semaj always answers the phone for me. Maybe she was still sleeping or something, being that it was early in the morning.

"Nigga, what?" I asked, remembering the nonsense Two just let fly out of his mouth.

"You heard me, shawty. Tell ya man that you ain't fucking with him anymore."

"First off, I don't have a man. Secondly, you're not about to be my man—"

"Yes, I am," he nodded, while keeping his eyes on the road. "I decided that shit last night."

"Man," I smacked my lips. "Don't tell me you're one of those crazy ass niggas that fall in love from fucking one time. I swear, y'all niggas annoying as fuck. Am I gonna have to cut you off?"

He let out a slight chuckle. "Nah. That's not me being crazy. That's me being determined."

I rolled my eyes. Men were always messing things up. All I wanted was someone to chill with and be able to have sex with them occasionally. I didn't want all the drama that came with a relationship. Shit, I didn't even want a relationship right now.

The rest of the ride to my place was a quiet one because I didn't have anything to say to him after that. I just felt like I was gonna have to cut him off because I wasn't going to deal with a crazy nigga. I didn't want him popping up when I was out, and I didn't want him trying to act a fool if he ever saw me out with another man. I didn't have time for it.

"Aight," he said as he pulled up in front of my apartment building. "I'ma call you and shit."

"Okay. I hear you." I muttered as I slid out the car.

"Aye," he called from behind me. I turned to look at him and he was already getting out of his car and doing a light jog towards me. "That's it? You not gon' give me a hug or nothing? You just gon' walk away like I wasn't all up in them guts last night?"

I sighed to myself. "You want a hug, Two?"

He nodded and held his arms out. "Hell yeah, shawty."

Slowly, I made my way back to him, where he pulled me right into his chest, and grabbed my face with his large hand. He didn't say a word as he gently placed his lips on mine.

"I said I'ma call you, aight?" he repeated, as he took a step away from me. "You better answer that shit, too."

I didn't say anything as he got in his car and drove away. He had me feeling some type of way, and I didn't like it. I wasn't trying to have feelings for any nigga. At least, not right now.

Once I was finally back into my apartment, I showered, threw on some clothes, fixed my hair, then was on my way to Semaj's place. I thought about calling her again, to let her know I was on my way, but I decided against it. I had a key to her house, so me calling really didn't matter.

My neighbor, who lived right across from me was standing in front of her door, smoking a cigarette. She was always in my business. I didn't even know her name, but she made sure to talk to me every time she saw me.

"Hey, Trinity," she smiled, as I looked up at her. She was a tall, brown skinned woman, probably in her early thirties. "I saw you get dropped off by your boyfriend, earlier." She had a small smirk on her face as I blew out a breath.

See what I mean? Always in my business.

"That wasn't my boyfriend." I said, as I walked away from her. Sometimes, she was okay to talk to, but other times, she annoyed the hell out of me. I tried to avoid her as much as I could.

On the ten-minute ride to Semaj's house, I found myself thinking about Two. He didn't seem like the relationship type at all. He seemed like he would tell me everything I wanted to hear while he was out there doing whatever the hell he wanted to do. Having sex with other women, and probably telling them some of the same things he was telling me.

"Oh no," I said to myself. "I don't have time for it."

My mouth fell open as I pulled up to Semaj's house. Or should I say what used to be her house. It was almost burned all the way to the ground, and that's when the panic started to set it.

This happened last night while I was getting some dick? Who did this? Was she in there when it happened? Is that why she didn't answer the phone when I'd called her earlier.

With my hands shaking and heart drumming against my chest, I dialed her number and patiently waited for her to answer. When I heard the voicemail again, I felt the tears stinging at my eyes.

I just sat there for a moment, not knowing what to think. That's when I remembered I had Tristan's number. I wasn't sure if he knew what was going on, but I was praying he told me some good news.

"What's up, ma?" he asked, sounding like he didn't have a car in the world.

"Hey, I know it's early, but have you seen or heard from Semaj? I'm at her place right now, and it's burned down. She's not answering the phone for me and I—"

"Yeah, I know exactly where she is. We're at one of her dad's houses."

I let out a loud sigh of relief. "Whew," I let out. "I thought my bitch was dead. I was about to get out the car and start rolling and screaming on the ground. Nigga, send me the damn address so I can come over there and cuss y'all both the fuck out."

"What? Why you—"

"Send me the address, Tristan!" I ended the call before he could respond, then seconds later, I got a message with the address.

I wasted no time putting the address in my GPS, then sped all the way over there. I'd never been to Dwayne's house when he was alive. Really, I only saw him once and that was back when we were in middle school. I couldn't imagine losing my dad. I probably would go crazy if I lost either one of my parents.

When I pulled up to the house, I was a little nervous of going in there. I didn't see Semaj's car out there, so I was starting to think he sent me the wrong address. I sat in my car for a little bit before I finally got out and walked towards the door. It swung open before I could even knock.

"You didn't get followed, did you?" Tristan asked, quickly closing the door.

"What? No, nobody followed me... Where's Semaj? What the hell happened to her house? Where's her car?"

"She's upstairs pouting. Long story short, though, somebody blew up her car, then burned her house down."

"Huh? Are you serious?"

"Dead ass. She hasn't said a word to me since last night. Maybe you can get her to talk to you." He shrugged as he slid his hands in his pockets, then I started up the stairs.

For some reason, I was shocked. I remember Antonio and Tristan saying something about people trying to kill Semaj, but I didn't know it was this bad.

"What the hell?" I muttered, once I was at the top of the stairs. It was a regular two-story house, but all the doors to every room was closed. Tristan could've at least told me which room to go to.

I sighed as I began for the closest door. It was a nice room. King sized bed, black covers, with a large TV mounted on the wall. But, there was no Semaj. So, I closed the door and started for the next room.

I wanted to jump for joy when I saw Semaj sitting on the bed, staring blankly at the TV.

"I know you're going through a lot right now, but you could've answered the phone when I called," I said, making my way to the bed. "And why the hell didn't you call me last night? Your whole house burned down and you didn't think to let anyone know?" I stood in front of her and folded my arms.

She slowly looked up at me. Eyes red and puffy, probably because she was up crying all, hair flying everywhere, and there was a gun sitting on her lap.

"My parents are dead," she said, quietly. "My dad killed my mom, then somebody killed him."

My brows came together. "He didn't kill your mom, Semaj—"

"He did," she nodded. "She was getting her drugs from him." I didn't know what to say. I didn't know that her dad was the person giving her mom the drugs. "Both my parents are dead. My house is gone, my car is gone. People want me dead for no reason. I didn't do anything to anyone, but they're trying to kill me?"

"Life comes at you fast, Semaj. I know things seem bad right now, but it'll all get better. You just have to give it time."

She scoffed. "Give it time? You think I need to give people trying to kill me time? Nah, fuck that shit. I'll probably make niggas happier if I was already dead."

I lifted an eyebrow. Semaj never said 'nigga'. Shit, she even hated when I said the word.

"Semaj, you're over there talking crazy. You're—"

She picked up the gun and put it to her head. I felt everything in my body freeze. I swear, everything was happening in slow motion as she pulled the trigger.

Click.

"Shit," she spat. "The fucking safety was on."

As she fumbled with the gun, I dove on the bed and snatched it from her.

"What the fuck, bruh?!" I hollered, fighting the urge to slap some sense into her ass. "Where the hell did you even get this from?!"

"Tristan gave it to me. He said I needed it."

"I'm sure he meant you needed it for protection! Not to try to kill yourself, bitch! I can't believe you — you know what?" I asked, getting of the bed and carefully placing the gun on the dresser. "Get the fuck up, Semaj. Let's go."

She threw her head back with a loud sigh. She already knew what was up.

"Come on, Trinity," she groaned. "Don't do this."

"No! You over there acting stupid as fuck. So, get the hell up. We're about to fight."

"Trinity—"

"Get the fuck up, Semaj!"

Semaj should've seen this coming. Whenever she would do some dumb shit, I would fight her. Yeah, I loved her to death, but sometimes, she just needed her ass beat.

She slowly pulled herself from the bed and came to stand in front of me.

"Trinity, I know what I just did was stupid, but—" My fist

connected with her nose. I didn't care about anything she had to say to me right now. "Ow! Trinity—" I hit her again. This time, I caught her in the mouth. "Stop it! Let me—" I slapped her as hard as I could. The look on her face let me know that she'd had enough. "Ugh!" she yelled, charging towards me.

The first thing she did was pull me by my hair and sling me to the floor. Semaj wasn't a fighter, but she could definitely beat a bitch up if she needed to. I wasn't about to let her beat me, though. Nope, not today. She needed this ass whoopin'.

I quickly got up and started swinging at her. She was trying to swing back, but I wasn't letting up. I was swinging at her like she had stolen something from me.

Usually, when me and Semaj would fight, I'd always feel like she learned her lesson when I started to see blood. Her nose was leaking, but this time I didn't care. She needed to know that I wasn't playing with her ass. What if the safety hadn't been on? She would've really killed herself right in front of me. That shit would've scarred me for life.

"Okay!" she yelled, backing away from me. "I've had enough, Trinity!"

"Nah," I laughed, flipping my hair out of my face. "You haven't!" I walked up on her, ready to swing on her again, but Tristan appeared at the door.

"The fuck are y'all doing?!" he yelled. I turned to look at him, and Semaj took that opportunity to jump on me.

"You know I don't like fighting!" she screamed, as she banged my head on the floor. I struggled underneath her.

"Bitch, get yo' heavy ass off me!"

"No," she huffed. "I'm not getting off until you tell me you're finished."

"I'm not finished! You deserve this ass whoopin', Semaj!"

Tristan pulled her off of me, and I quickly stood to my feet.

"Yo, what the fuck are y'all fighting for? This ain't—"

"Nigga, your dumb ass cousin just tried to kill herself! Her stupid ass still had the damn safety on! Why the fuck would you even give her a gun?" I yelled, now walking up on him. At this point, I was ready to give him these hands, too.

"What? Man, I gave her the gun for protection! The fuck, Semaj?" He turned in her direction, then glared at her like she was a child in trouble.

"Okay, fuck both of y'all! I don't wanna live my life like this! I don't wanna be afraid all the time! I don't like this hood shit! That's why I spent all these years burying it!" She wiped her nose with the back of her hand, then shot me a look.

Yeah, bitch. I busted your nose. I bet you won't run up, though.

"You were born into this hood shit, Semaj! You ran from that shit like it was a fuckin' disease, but now look. The shit came back to bite you in the ass, and now you don't know how to fuckin' act."

She shook her head. "No!"

"So, what you gon' do? You gon' kill yourself because you're afraid? Then what, Semaj? You gonna be happy then?"

She shrugged. "I don't know, Tristan. I'm gonna be dead."

"That's some real dumb shit, Semaj," he let her know. "Niggas die every day. If that's what you wanna do, then do it." He walked over to the dresser, retrieved the gun, then handed it to her. "Go ahead. You 'bout it, ain't you?"

Semaj looked down at the gun that was now in her hand, then let out a small chuckle.

"Fuck both of y'all," she spat, tossing the gun on the floor, then grabbing her purse, and walked out the room.

I thought about going to follow her, but I quickly decided against it. She needed this time to cool off, so I was gonna let her.

After a few moments, we heard the front door slam. Tristan let out a loud sigh.

"This shit is gonna be way harder than I expected," he said.

8

TRAP

"You know, my mom asked what college you went to today,"
Jordyn laughed as she rode happily in the passenger seat. "I was like
'girl, I only date drug dealers and thugs'." She flipped her hair from her
shoulder as I glanced at her.

"First off, we ain't dating," I let her know. "Secondly, I'm not a drug
dealer. Don't be going around telling people that shit."

"Not dating?" she flipped. "Boy, you're taking me on a date
right now."

"Nah. You hit me up asking if I wanted to go to the bar and I said
yeah. There ain't nothing more to it, shawty."

She looked at me for a moment, not knowing what to say. She was
probably going around telling people we were dating which was a fat
ass lie. I couldn't date a girl like Jordyn. She was too childish for me.

"What you mean you're not a drug dealer?" she asked, switching
the subject.

"Exactly what the fuck I said. I don't sell drugs."

"Then, what do you do? I mean, you just look like a drug dealer to
me. You've got the tattoos, the beard, and the hair. Don't think I didn't

peep the pistol sitting in your lap, either. Everything about you screams drug dealer."

I chuckled lightly to myself. "Damn, ma. You stereotyping the hell outta me. Does it bother you that I'm not a drug dealer? You sounding a little disappointed over there."

"I mean, no," she said, shaking her head. "I was drawn to you because I thought you were a drug dealer. What are you, then?"

"A killer," I said, easily.

Her eyes lit up as she looked at me. "Really? That's even better!"

This bitch was weird as hell. She was still talking to me, but I tuned her ass out until I pulled into the parking lot. All I wanted to do was get a few drinks, pay for her ass an Uber, then take my ass home. I could tell she had other plans, but she was about to be in for a rude awakening.

"I'm so glad you agreed to come with me," she boasted as we got out the car.

"Mhm," I responded, making my way towards the door.

"We're gonna have so much fun. I'm always fun to hang around."

She was talking too damn much. She'd been talking since I picked her overly happy ass up.

Once I was inside the bar, I did a quick scan, making sure I didn't see anything out the ordinary. When I was finished with that, I went to sit down at one of the booths.

"So, is your real name Trap?" Jordyn asked as she sat down in front of me.

I shook my head. "Nah, but that's what you can call me."

She twisted her face up a little. "What if I don't wanna call you Trap? What does your mom call you?"

"Damn, you all up in my business." I laughed. "I said you can call me Trap."

She rolled her eyes. "That's not fair."

I shrugged. I didn't really give a damn.

"So, then," I heard, coming from the table behind me. "The fuckin' funeral got shot up. First, I get my ass beat, now people are shooting?"

I didn't have to turn around to know who was talking. Shit, now that I knew she was here, I'd rather be talking to her instead of Jordyn.

"So, lemme get this straight," some nigga said. "Your dad left you all his money and businesses, and now you got people trying to kill you?"

"Yep. They burned my house down and blew my car to pieces. I worked hard for my shit, too."

Damn. Shawty sounded like she had a rough couple of days.

"You hear me, Trap?" Jordyn said, making me remember she was sitting in front of me.

"Nah."

"I said I was going to get me a drink. You want anything?"

"Yeah. Get me a beer."

She smiled as she slid out the booth. "I knew that's what you were gonna drink,"

As soon as she had her back turned, I got up and invited myself to sit next to Semaj. She looked at me like I was crazy, but that shit didn't bother me.

"What's up, Semmy?" I asked, looking at the square ass nigga she was here with. He was eyeing me like he wanted to say something, but he was too pussy to say it. Nigga looked familiar as fuck, too.

"Um, Mega, I'm clearly on a date. It's pretty rude how—"

"A date? You dating married men now?" I asked, looking at the gold wedding ring that was on his finger.

That's when I remembered where I knew the nigga from. He was Two's lawyer once, and I was fucking his wife.

"Huh?" Semaj asked, with her brows coming together. "He's not married." She was so confident with her answer, which caused me to laugh.

"I know you see that man's ring, Semmy. I know you see it."

She looked down at his hands, and he quickly tried to hide them.

"Wow," she laughed. "So, that's why you wouldn't be in a relationship with me, Marcus? Because you have a fuckin' wife?"

"Semaj, it's not like—"

"Y'all got kids, too?"

I laughed to myself as the guilt played out on his face. Shit was priceless.

"Trap?" Jordyn asked, standing next to me with our drinks in her hands. "What are you doing?"

"What it look like I'm doing? I'm talking. Go sit down." She glared at me, then at Semaj, but she went and sat her ass down.

"You can leave now," Semaj said to that square ass nigga. "There's no point of you still sitting here."

"You asked me to come here with you, Semaj."

"Okay? And now I'm asking you to leave. Good bye."

He shook his head. "Look, Semaj. We can talk about this like two adults. I don't know who your friend is, but—"

She threw the rest of her drink in his face, then threw the cup at him, too.

"I said get the fuck on, nigga!" she yelled, sounding like she was straight out of North Atlanta. "Ain't shit to talk about, bruh! You just another bitch ass nigga that wasted my time. Fuck outta here." She didn't sound like that same proper ass white girl anymore. Nah, her true colors were showing now.

"Nigga?" he asked, standing up like his bitch ass was offended. "Now, I may be a lot of things, but I am not a nigg—"

"She said leave, bruh!" I snapped. "Fuck you still standing here for?"

He didn't say anything as he turned to leave. I looked at Semaj who ran her fingers through her hair.

"I'm sorry that I just acted like that in a public place," she said, sounding like her normal self again. "I'm going through a lot right now and... You know what? I think I should just leave."

"Nah. Stay yo' ass right here. I'll be right back." I got up and made my way back to Jordyn who was giving me the look of death.

"About time, nigga," she sneered. "Who the hell is she, and why are you giving her so much attention when you came here with me?"

"Aye, check this out," I said, pulling a twenty from my wallet. "Call yourself an Uber. I'll get up with you later."

Her mouth fell open. "Huh? You brought me all the way here just to ditch me for another woman?" She was talking louder than I wanted her to.

"I said I'll get up with you later, bruh. You better be glad I'm even paying for this shit."

I grabbed the beer she'd purchased for me, then went to sit in front of Semaj. She looked like she was stressing.

"Yo, what's up? Why every time I see you, you look like you just got into a fight?"

"Because, I did," she sighed.

"Damn. Again? Who you fighting now?"

"My best friend. I did something stupid earlier, so she fought me."

"What? What kinda best friend you got?"

"A crazy one."

I nodded. "What the hell you do to make her that mad?"

She looked down at her hands like she didn't wanna answer me.

"I tried to kill myself." she said quietly.

I lifted a brow. "How?"

"My cousin gave me a gun for protection, so I put it to my head, pulled the trigger, but the safety was on. She was standing there the entire time I did it. So, then she got mad at me and we fought."

"Man, what the fuck you tryna kill yourself for, shawty? Ain't no way your life is that bad."

She let out a breath. "Well, both my parents are dead, my dad left everything he owned to me, my family are all trying to kill me now, and I no longer have a car or a house because they destroyed it. I got my ass beat and shot at while I was at my daddy's funeral. This isn't the life I want," she shook her head.

"I get shot at damn near every day, ma. You don't see me crying over that shit."

"Okay, but you're used to it. I'm not. I don't like—"

"You were raised in one of those white ass neighborhoods?"

"No. I wish," she muttered.

"You were raised in the hood?"

She nodded. "That's all my mama could afford." There wasn't anything wrong with that. I was born and raised in the hood.

"True shit. How ya moms die?"

"Well, she'd been addicted to drugs since I was little, so she over-dosed. Over the years, her addiction got worse and worse."

Damn.

"Shit. So, you had to live with your pops after that?"

She chuckled. "Hell no. That man never came around. He didn't even come to the funeral, being that he was the one who killed her in the first place."

"Word? He was selling her that shit?"

"Yep. I still can't believe it. My family sucks. Now, they're all trying to kill me because they want the money. It's crazy how money can make people act so crazy."

"Aye," I shrugged. "It be like that sometimes. Money will make a mothafucka forget y'all even came from the same bloodline."

She was quiet for a moment. "I just don't understand why my cousin gave me a gun. I don't even know how to use it." she sighed to herself.

"Shit, it ain't that hard. You just aim it, and BOW! Let that motha-fucka off. Blow a nigga's head right off his shoulders."

She let out a shrill laugh. "Goodness. I didn't expect you to do that."

I smiled at her pretty ass. She didn't have an ounce of makeup on, but still looked like she belonged on the cover of a magazine.

"You afraid of guns?" I questioned, watching her nod her head.

"Yes. I'm even afraid to hold them. They feel so... dangerous."

"Once you learn how to use them, you won't feel like that anymore. You just gotta learn to use them."

"Mhm," she said, flipping her hair. "What made you want to get tattoos on your face?" I could tell by the tone of her voice that she didn't like them. I didn't really give a fuck, though. I didn't get tatted to please her ass.

"I ran outta space everywhere else," I chuckled. "You don't fuck with them?"

"No. I don't like tattoos at all. I'm amazed at how many you have. They didn't hurt?"

"Hell nah. I don't ever feel shit. Except on my fingers," I said, holding one of my hands up. "That shit almost made a nigga cry,"

She giggled as she grabbed my hand to examine it. "You like music?"

"Nah, but I liked the way the music notes looked, so I got them bitches tatted."

She nodded with a small laugh. "Can I ask you something? I don't want you to judge me or anything."

"I don't judge nobody, shawty."

"Great. Can you teach me how to shoot?"

9

SEMAJ

I didn't expect to run into Mega at the bar. Really, I was only here to get away from everyone, but I was glad he showed up.

Finding out Marcus was married came as a shock to me, but at the same time, nothing shocked me when it came to him. I wanted to be sad, but for what? What was the point?

Today, Mega looked… different. He had his hair in four braids going straight back, two large diamond earrings in both ears, and a simple white shirt with some jeans on. I didn't want to admit it, but he looked cute.

He kept smiling at me, showing off his perfect teeth. I didn't know if it was because I'd been drinking a little bit or what, but he was making my lady parts go crazy. I was beyond grateful that he said he would teach me how to shoot, but first, I had to drop Tristan's car off.

"Can you follow behind me? I need to give my cousin his car back," I said as we walked out the bar.

"Hell yeah. I ain't got shit to do anyway."

He made me nervous. I didn't even feel like this when I was around Marcus. I scoffed just thinking about him. What I should do is find out who the hell his wife was and let her know that he was cheating on her, but that would take too much energy.

Even though I wasn't really feeling Trinity right now, I couldn't wait to let her know what happened. Knowing her, she's probably just gonna say, "I told you so," and make me feel dumber than I already did. I just couldn't understand how I never paid attention to his ring until today.

As I was driving, I kept glancing in my rearview mirror to look at Mega. It was a little hard to believe that this was happening right now. I couldn't believe he was casually following behind me, and my nerves were this bad.

"He's definitely not even my type." I said aloud to myself. After he showed me how to shoot, I probably wouldn't talk to him ever again. Yeah, that sounded like a good plan.

When I pulled up to the house, I quickly parked in the driveway, then did a light jog to the front door. Luckily, no one was downstairs when I walked in. I wasn't in the mood to talk to anyone right now, anyway.

Once I sat the keys down on the table, I hurried back outside and into Mega's car.

"Okay," I huffed out of breath. "We can leave now."

We pulled off, and my phone vibrated in my hand. I looked down at it, only to see a text from Marcus, which caused me to roll my eyes.

Marcus: Call me when you have a chance

I definitely wasn't going to do that. I didn't have anything to say to him. I still couldn't believe I'd fell for his lies.

"Aye," Mega said, causing me to glance at him. "I know this does have anything to do with what's going on, but you got a fat ass. That shit—"

"Excuse me?!" I snapped, eyes widening in shock. "Why are you looking at my—"

"Man, chill with that wannabe white girl shit. We both grown, you got a fat ass, so I'ma look."

I rolled my eyes. Men were so annoying.

"Well, I'd appreciate if you didn't look at my ass, Mega. Thank you."

He let out a laugh like I'd just told the funniest joke. "Hell nah. I'm looking at that shit every chance I get. There's no way that square ass nigga was hitting that shit right. Ain't no fuckin' way, bruh."

"Me and Marcus' sex life is none of your damn business."

He smiled at me. "That shit was whack, wasn't it?"

"No," I quickly defended. But, then I realized, the sex was whack. Marcus never wanted to do what I wanted him to do. We always did the same position. "I mean… it was okay."

"Nah, shawty. Shit was whack. You don't gotta lie."

"I'm not lying."

"You loved that nigga or something? How long were you his side hoe?"

I smacked my lips and flipped my hair off my shoulder. "Okay, first off, Mega, I wasn't anyone's side hoe. Just because—"

"Nah," he nodded. "You were his side. He had a whole wife. I mean, she was cheating on his ass too, but—"

"What? How would you even know that?" I questioned, looking at him as his focused his attention on the road.

"Because I fucked her a few times. Shit was aight. She was too damn old to not know how to suck dick. She was the type of bitch to only put the tip in her mouth and shit. What kinda—"

"I really don't wanna hear about your sexual encounters with other women, Mega."

"Why not? Man, I got some crazy ass stories. I was fucking with a bitch who didn't like to shave, and bruh," he flipped. "That shit was like a jungle. Why the—"

"Mega? Please. I really don't wanna hear it. Talk about something else."

"So, it's either your way or the highway, huh?"

I crossed my arms. "No, it's not that at all. How would you feel about hearing me talk about sex with another man?"

He shrugged. "Shit, it would probably be funny because I know all of your sexual experiences were whack."

"No, they weren't! I've had great sex, before. You don't know shit."

"Why you so defensive? I've fucked some bitches before and the shit was whack. It's life."

I didn't have anything to say back to him, so I just kept quiet. I didn't know why I even asked him to teach me to shoot. Didn't know what the hell I was thinking.

"Where are you taking me?" I asked, once I noticed we were on a back road, with nothing but trees surrounding it.

"You wanna learn how to shoot, right?"

I nodded. "Yeah, but—"

"Then shut the hell up. You think I'ma kidnap your annoying ass?"

Annoying?

"I mean, I don't know what you're capable of." With the events that happened within the last few days, I didn't trust anyone. On top of that, I'd told Mega about my dad leaving me everything, so he could be feeling the same way my family was feeling.

Shit. Why did I get myself into this?

I didn't know anything about Mega. I didn't know what he did for a living, or if he had mental problems or not.

"You don't wanna know what I'm capable of, Semmy." he let me know with a wink.

I wasn't sure if he was flirting with me, or if he was being serious. All I knew was, any man that could get tattoos on his face was crazy. End of story.

Once again, I didn't have anything to say, so we fell into an awkward silence. I wasn't sure if he knew this or not, but I was scared. I just knew he was going to kill me, then dump my body in the woods somewhere. No one was going to know what happened to me.

Fuck.

It seemed like we drove for another hour, but finally, we pulled up to what looked like an abandoned warehouse, and my heart sank to the pit of my stomach.

No one would be able to hear my screams, and even if I called the police, by the time they got here, it would be too late.

He parked, turned the car off, then looked at me. "You ready?"

I slowly nodded, but I wasn't ready. I wasn't ready to lose my life. Not yet.

Once he got out the car, I followed behind him.

"Oh nah," he said, looking at me. "Leave your purse in the car. Leave your phone, too. you won't need that shit in here."

I hesitated for a moment, but I finally put my purse down in the seat, then closed the door. My legs felt like noodles as I slowly followed behind him. I could hear my heart beating in my ears, and I was starting to sweat in places that I wasn't supposed to sweat in.

"Aight," he said as he opened the door. "I'm gonna start you off with something small. Your first lesson isn't gonna be too rough on you." We walked into a large room, and he cut on the light.

There were guns everywhere. It almost looked like something out of a movie. I felt like a kid in a candy store looking around at all the guns that were hanging on the wall. Some were on the table that was in the middle of the floor.

"Goodness," I muttered to myself.

"Here," he said, shoving a small gun in my face. "It's a .380. You should be able to handle it." It looked identical to the one Tristan had given me, but smaller.

Mega then walked over to another door and opened it. I followed right behind him before he could tell me to. Once I was through the door, I regretted it. I wanted to turn around and run out, but my legs wouldn't move.

"You ain't scared, are you?" he asked, once he saw my facial expression.

"No," I lied, shaking my head. Clearly, I was scared. I didn't even know why he was asking stupid questions.

There was a guy, badly beaten, and tied to a chair just sitting in the middle of the floor. I glanced at Mega who had a wicked smile on his face as he walked over to the man, then pulled his gun out.

"Get yo' bitch ass up, nigga!" he yelled, smacking him in the face with the gun. I cringed at the sound it made. I didn't want to be here anymore.

The man groaned as he looked up at Mega. "Damn, you still ain't killed me, yet?" he asked with a small chuckle.

"Nah, but I'm 'bout to." Mega came and stood next to me. "Shoot him."

"Huh? But why? He didn't do anything to me. I don't even know him." I said, with the gun trembling in my hand.

"I didn't ask you if you knew him, Semaj. I told you to shoot him. What you waiting on?"

"You didn't tell me I was going to hurt someone, Mega."

He shrugged. "You didn't ask."

"So, you just go around kidnapping people? Then, kill them? Is that what you're gonna do to me after this? Tie me up and torture me?" I folded my arms as I looked at him.

"Shoot the nigga, Semaj. Why you talking so much?"

"Because I don't feel right doing this! I already don't know how to shoot, but now you're wanting me to shoot an innocent person? What the hell is that?"

He pulled an aggravated hand down his face. "He ain't innocent, shawty. Molesting kids ain't innocent. Shoot this man so I can see where your aim is at."

I sighed and aimed the gun. My hands were still shaking, but I as trying my hardest to get them to stop. I closed my eyes and pulled the trigger, only for the gun to click loudly.

"Bruh," Mega laughed. "The safety should be the first thing you always look at when you get a gun. What if this nigga was about to kill you? That would've been it. Lights out for yo' ass."

"I just thought you would've already taken the safety off." I said quietly.

"Don't ever think no shit like that. Do you even know how to take the safety off?"

"Yes," I scoffed. "I know how to do that." I quickly took the safety off and aimed the gun at him again. The guy in the chair looked dead at me, then gave me a small smile.

I planned to shoot him in his head, but as I squeezed the trigger, the bullet hit him in his chest, and my stomach weakened.

"Do it again," Mega demanded.

I was still trying to get myself together from what I'd just saw, but I pulled the trigger again. This time, I hit him in his shoulder, and he cried out in pain. He was coughing up blood, looking like he was gonna die at any minute, and I felt tears stinging in my eyes.

"I don't wanna kill him," I retorted, trying to hand him the gun.

"So, what you gon' do when one of ya family members run up on you shooting and shit? You gonna fold like a little hoe?"

"That's different! I don't even know this man!"

"Shoot him, Semaj. Don't think, just do it."

I shook my head. "I can't."

He shrugged. "Either way he gon' die, shawty. Either you can speed that shit up, or you can make his ass suffer."

I looked back at the guy. Mega was right. There was no way he was going to survive with two bullet wounds in him like that. I knew for a fact that Mega wasn't going to take him to a hospital so he could get treated.

"Fuck," I sighed to myself, aiming the gun for the last time. This time when I pulled the trigger, I hit him right in his forehead, and I watched the blood splatter all over the place. "Oh my God," I said, covering my mouth.

"Oh shit," Mega said, walking closer to me. "That wasn't too bad for your first lesson."

"I'm gonna fuckin' throw up." I said, pushing Mega away from me. I quickly looked around the room to see if there was a trashcan anywhere, but there wasn't one.

"Come on, Semaj. I know your stomach stronger that." But, it wasn't. I leaned over and threw up everything I had consumed that day.

At that moment, I felt so weak. I could barely stand up, and I really felt like I was gonna pass out.

"See man, I wanna help you, but you probably smell like throw up." Mega said as I looked up at him.

"Can you take me home please?"

"I mean yeah… you good, though? You not gon' throw up no more are you?"

I cut my eyes at him. "Mega, take me home. I'm not gonna throw up in your damn car."

"Yeah, you say that, but you over there looking like you got a little more left in you. I'm just saying. I don't wanna be cleaning up no damn throw up outta my car. Shit," He took the gun from me and started to walk away.

When I asked him to teach me how to shoot, this was not what I had in mind. Actually, I didn't know what I had in mind. I didn't think I would have to kill someone today. Someone that I'd never even met before.

"Can't even believe this," I muttered as I slid into the passenger seat. "Where are we even at? You really had to drag me all the way out here to teach me how to shoot? Why couldn't we just go to the shooting range or something?" I looked at Mega, then watched as he got out the car and went around to the trunk. He returned as quickly as he left.

"No, offense, but your breath stinks." He handed me a large bottle of mouthwash and I looked at him like he was crazy.

"So, you just ride around with mouthwash in your trunk?" I raised an amused brow.

"Hell yeah. You never know what might happen. I got hella tooth brushes too."

Instead of questioning his logic, I twisted the cap open and rinsed my mouth out with it. I wanted to run my mouth some more, but I was beyond grateful that he had mouthwash with him. I knew my breath smelled bad, and this wasn't the last impression I wanted to have on him.

"Thank you," I said, once I was finished.

"That feeling should go away. The more you kill, the easier it gets."

My eyes widened. "You think I'm just gonna be walking around killing innocent people for no reason?"

"That nigga you just killed wasn't innocent, though." He started the car and pulled off.

"Why did you have him chained up like that, though? What did he do to you?" I was almost too afraid to ask, but I had to know. It wasn't normal to just have someone tied up in an abandoned warehouse.

"He stole some shit from me and thought I wouldn't find out." he said, easily. For some reason, that didn't make me feel better at all.

So, someone steals from you, so you tie them up? Maybe what he stole was really important. I wanted to ask, but I didn't want him to think I was all up in his business.

"Oh," I said after a while. At this point, I just wanted to get home and forget about everything that had just happened. I was trying to play it cool, but right now I was actually terrified of Mega.

He was crazy. There was no questioning it, now. I couldn't wait to get away from him, then never talk to his ass ever again.

10

TWO

"Nigga, you probably scarred that girl for life," I said to Trap as we made our way to the locker room. At least once a week, me, Trap, and our nigga Spazz would come to the gym and play basketball, while making a few niggas mad in the process because they couldn't see us on the court. Today was no different. Same shit happened.

"Nah, she good. She's the one who asked me to teach her how to shoot." Trap said with a small shrug. Nigga was stupid as fuck.

"Yeah, that means you take her to a shooting range or some shit. You full live made her kill a mothafucka. Man, she probably cried all night after that."

"Man, I'm tryna tell you that shawty was good. She wasn't acting weird or anything. I mean, after she bodied dude, she threw up a little bit, but it was nothing major."

"Damn," I laughed. "She ain't gonna want shit to do with you after that. You haven't talked to her since then, have you?"

"I mean, nah, but that's probably because she's busy. You know I'm not the type of nigga to text all day, anyway."

"So, you didn't call her to check up on her or anything?" Spazz chimed in. His ass was so quiet half the time, I would forget that he was even there.

"Nah. Was I supposed to? She's a grown ass woman."

"But you exposed her to some shit she's not used to seeing. She didn't grow up in the streets like us. You can tell by how she talks like a white girl," I let him know.

"Nah. She's from the hood."

"No she ain't," I chuckled. "Ain't no way she's from the—"

"Her mom was a crackhead. What crackhead you know lives in the suburbs?"

"Shit, I know a few."

"Who is this chick? Do I know her?" Spazz questioned as we all got our shit together.

"Dwayne's daughter. I thought that nigga had a son this whole time," I said.

"Oh shit, you fuckin' her?" he asked, turning his attention to Trap. "Wasn't you the one who killed—"

"I'm not fucking her," Trap spat.

"Yeah, but you want to. You can't go five minutes without bringing her ass up."

"Man, hell nah. Leave that bitch alone. It's gonna end badly," Spazz warned, but Trap was already shaking his head.

"I'm a grown ass man. I'ma do whatever the fuck I want—"

"Nigga, you killed the girl's dad. Y'all gon' start fuckin', you gon' fall in love with the pussy, everything's gonna be sweet for a little bit, then boom. She finds out you killed her dad, and it's lights out or you." I said, as we walked out the locker room.

"Nigga, ain't nobody gonna fall in love with the pussy. I'm good."

"Remember Mona?" I asked. "That dark skinned bitch that was stealing shit from you every time you brought her ass around?"

He smacked his lips. "Why you always bringing up old shit, yo?"

"Because you always falling for dumb bitches. How you let a bitch rob you? I still can't believe that shit."

He glanced at me. "Semaj ain't like that, though. She wouldn't find out what I did to her pops, but even if she did, she wouldn't do shit. I would just explain to her ass that it wasn't anything personal. It's just my job." He shrugged like the shit would be that easy and I shook my head. Trap never had the best luck with bitches. Something always went wrong.

"Whatever, nigga. Don't call me when that bitch sending bullets through yo' ass."

He didn't say anything as we walked through the doors. All three of us stopped in our tracks when we saw all the niggas we'd just played ball with, and plus some, standing out front, waiting for us.

See, I knew a few of these niggas looked familiar. These eastside niggas got on my nerves.

"What's up?" Trap asked, dropping everything he had in his hands to the ground.

"You already know what's up, nigga," the light skinned nigga with dreads said, taking a step forward.

I looked at every nigga that was standing around us. There were eight of them, and three of us. We were outnumbered like shit, but I didn't give a fuck. I wanted to beat the fuck outta this light skinned nigga.

"Y'all really tryna do this shit right now?" Spazz asked, pulling his pants up. he was a quiet ass nigga, but fighting was one of his favorite things to do.

"Hell yeah, nigga! Y'all started this war! Don't try and act pussy now!" light skinned yelled.

I didn't care about all the talking that was going on. Yeah, it might've been my fault that there was now a war going on between us and the eastside niggas, but clearly, I didn't give a fuck.

There had always been problems between westside and eastside, but if you ask me, they're the ones who brought this shit on themselves.

It was a regular ass day and shit, and I was minding my business, walking into the corner store, getting me a cigarillo so I could smoke. I got my shit, then walked back to my car. But, before I could even get to my car, there was a gun being pressed into the back of my head, and a nigga telling me to give them all my money.

Immediately, I was pissed. I was being robbed and broad daylight, and I left my strap in the car.

I gave him everything I had in my pockets, then watched his bitch ass run off. I didn't know who the fuck that nigga thought I was, but I spent the rest of that day looking for him. Trap tried to tell me I was doing too much, but nah, I wasn't. He would've been on the same shit if it happened to him.

We finally found the nigga, walking around downtown with some bitch. He looked like he was having the time of his life, thinking shit was sweet. We pulled up on his ass, and I shot him two times in the chest, and once in the head. I thought about killing the bitch, too, but I decided against it. I told her to let them eastside niggas know that Two did it.

Of course, her scary ass told everyone, which started a war between west side and eastside. Now, here we were, about to get jumped, but it was all good. I was about to have fun with this shit.

"Aye," I said, getting the light skinned nigga's attention. "How ya moms been doing?"

He screwed his face up. "Fuck that gotta do with you, nigga?"

"4243 Vine street? She still live in the house with the red shutters, right?"

"The fuck? Swear to God, you touch my mama, I'ma—"

"You ain't gon' do shit nigga. I'll body yo' ass just like I did your brother. Leave ya moms with no kids at all." Yeah, his brother was the little nigga that robbed me. I didn't know what the fuck their names were because I wasn't good with names, but that shit didn't matter. I knew their faces and shit.

Before he could say anything back, an all-black Altima pulled up, then rolled the window down. I swear everything was happening in slow motion as I watched the nigga roll his window down and aim his pistol at us.

"Eastside nigga!" he yelled, as he let off his gun.

I tried to run for cover, but before I could get away, I was hit in the shoulder and fell to the ground.

"Fuck!" I yelled, holding my shoulder. I'd been shot before, and I knew one thing; I never wanted to get shot again. Clearly, shit didn't always work out the way you wanted it to.

"Come on, nigga!" Trap said, helping me up from the ground. "Let's go!"

The Altima sped off and we quickly made our way to the car.

"You would get shot today," Spazz laughed once we were in the car.

"Nigga fuck you," I spat. "Mothafuckas ain't gon' be happy until I kill every single last one of those eastside niggas."

"Damn, man. You getting blood all over my shit," Trap complained.

"Well drive faster! I don't know why you're driving like I'm not back here leaking anyway!"

"Man, you get grumpy as fuck when you get shot." Spazz said, still laughing. If I hadn't been in so much pain at that moment, I would've hit that nigga in the back of his head.

About two hours later, I was all bandaged up and was sitting on my couch waiting for this little shawty that I knew to come over. The hospital was trying to make me stay overnight, but I wasn't going for that shit.

I only got shot in my shoulder, so I was good. They were tryna make it into something it wasn't. Then, they had the police all up in that bitch, trying to ask me questions and shit. Fuck that. I didn't talk to the pigs.

My phone rang beside me, causing me to put the blunt down that I was about to light, so I could answer it.

"Yooo,"

"Oh, so you're alive, huh?" Trinity snapped. I told her I was gonna call her ass right back, but that had been a week ago.

"Shit, my bad, ma. A nigga been busy and shit."

She let out a small chuckle. "I bet you have. This is the reason I don't take niggas serious. Y'all ain't shit."

"Man, chill with all that shit. We're talking now, so that's all that matters."

"Boy, bye. I'm about to hang up. I just called to see if you were alive. Now that I know you are, I'm not—"

"You want some dick, don't you?" The phone was quiet for a minute. I knew her ass didn't hang up. She was calling for a reason.

"I mean, I wanted dick like a week ago, but you've been busy so—"

"Man, shut that shit up. You doing anything later? You know you wanna come over."

She smacked her lips. "No, I'm not doing anything, but who said I wanted to come over?"

"You did. That's why you called, right? You didn't just call to talk shit, did you? You ain't one of those bitches, right?"

"First off, nigga, don't call me a bitch. Yeah, I called because I wanted dick, but now—"

"I'll call you when you can come, shawty." I ended the call before she could respond. She wanted to argue, and that's not the type of shit that I was on.

As soon as I tossed the phone back on the couch, there was a knock at the door. I knew exactly who it was.

"Sorry I took so long," she said, once I opened the door. "I had to drive my brother around since he doesn't have a car. You know how that goes."

She stepped into the house, and I closed the door.

"Nah, I don't. I always got a car. I'm not a bum ass nigga like your brother. What's up, though?" She flipped her weave, then looked at me.

I started fucking with Destiny a while ago, when she was still ugly. At first, she used to steal money and weed from her brother for me, and I would break her ass off with some dick.

That went on for a couple of months until she ended up pregnant by some other nigga, so I cut her off. I didn't care that she was pregnant, but she was the one saying we couldn't fuck anymore since she was pregnant. If we weren't fucking, the there was no reason to keep her around, so I didn't. I dropped her ass like a bad habit. About a month ago, she was in a really bad car accident, which caused her to lose the baby. That shit was fucked up, too.

She called me earlier today, letting me know she wanted to give me something, so I told her to slide through.

"What happened to your shoulder?" she asked, sitting down on the couch.

"Got shot earlier by a pussy nigga," I said easily.

"Seriously?! Are you okay?"

"Don't I look okay?"

"I mean, yeah, but you never know. Do you know who did it?"

"Nah, but you already know I'm gon' find out. Fuck I look like?"

She rolled her eyes. "You need to calm down, Two. One day, you're gonna really gonna get hurt. What am I gonna do if you end up dying?"

"You're probably gonna go on with your life, shawty. Let's be real."

Destiny always talked like she was my girlfriend and shit. I'd told her multiple times that I didn't want a damn relationship with her ass, but she would always ignore me.

Like I said, Destiny was ugly when I first met her. Her hair was short and brittle, she had pimples and acne scars all over her face, and she couldn't dress to save her life. She looked like a straight bum when we first met. But, once she started seeing the other bitches I was fucking with, she decided to step her game up.

She started dressing better, started getting her hair done and shit, and she started doing something to her face because her acne and shit looked like it was clearing up.

"Okay, so you know about the accident I was in, right?" she started, as I sat down. "And I lost my baby."

"Yeah, I know." I said, ready for her to get on with whatever it was she had to say.

"Well, I got paid for that. A hundred thousand dollars." She gave me a small smile and I was trying to figure out what the hell she was telling me this shit for. I mean, the shit was good, since she lost her baby and shit, but so the fuck what? What did that shit have to do with me?

"Okay?" I finally said, looking at her.

"Since you've been the only person who cares about me, and listens to me when I talk, I wanna give a little bit to you." she said, causing me to lift an eyebrow.

"Word? I mean, I'm not gonna tell you not to."

"Right. So, I was thinking twenty thousand. Does that sound good to you?" Does it sound good? Was this bitch stupid? That shit sounded lovely.

"Shit, whatever you wanna do," I said, trying to play it cool. I didn't wanna seem too eager even though I was geekin' on the inside.

"Good," she smiled. "Now, you know what I want from you, right?" She gave me a look of lust, and I knew exactly what she wanted.

"Come on," I said, walking in the direction of my room. I wanted to do some smooth shit and pick her ass up to take her to the room, but with my shoulder fucked up like this, I knew that shit wouldn't have worked.

As we made our way to my room, Trinity flashed through my mind. She was probably gonna be mad as shit, but she would just have to wait.

"I've been thinking about this for a while," Destiny said, taking her shirt off, and tossing it to the floor. "I haven't met a nigga that can fuck better than you can."

All shawty was doing was feeding my ego. She was about to get the best dick of her life because of what she just did. I didn't even feel bad about doing it, either.

"You sure you can do this?" she asked, once she seen that I was in pain.

"I'm good, ma. Lay yo' ass down."

"But you look like you're struggling over there. I can help you if you want." I shook my head. She was starting to piss me off with all her questions and shit. I got this. I was a grown ass man. I could do the shit by my damn self.

"I said I got it, Destiny."

I could tell by the look on her face that she didn't believe me. I ignored the look she was giving me and managed to get my pants down with one hand.

"You wanna take some more medicine?" she questioned, making me cut my eyes at her.

I sighed to myself. "Yeah, I can take some more pills."

After I took some more medicine, everything was a blur. The only thing I remember was waking up and Destiny kissing me all over my face.

"Good morning," she smiled. "I put yo' ass to sleep last night."

Damn, morning? I didn't even mean to pass out like that.

"Shit," I said, sitting up in bed. "I don't even remember shit."

"I do. It was great, just like always. I gotta go, though. I'll wire the money to your account as soon as I get home."

She kissed me again, then left out the room before I could say anything. My shoulder felt like it was on fire, but I was too tired to even get up and take medicine. Once I heard the front door close, I closed my eyes again. I wasn't starting my day no time soon. I'm gonna stay my ass in this same spot all day.

11

TRINITY

"So, where the hell you been for the past week, Semaj?" I asked, watching her stick a fork full of Chinese food in her mouth.

"I've been getting my thoughts together. There was just too much going on last week. People trying to kill me, my house burning down, my car blowing up, killing someone that I didn't even know—"

"Hold on, what?"

She sighed to herself. "It's a long story."

"Okay? Well make that shit short, then. What the hell did you do after you stormed out the house?"

"I went to a bar with Marcus and had a few drinks. Nothing major."

"A few drinks? Since when do you drink anything besides wine?"

"You gonna let me tell the story or what?"

I lifted a brow. "Go ahead."

"Okay, so I'm there with Marcus, and Mega shows up with his female companion. They sit directly behind us."

"Mega?" I asked. "You talking about Trap?"

"Mhm," she says while rolling her eyes. "So, he comes to my table and sits next to me like we're just the best of friends, and I politely tell him I'm on a date because I freakin' was."

Now, it was my turn to roll my eyes. She really needed to leave Marcus alone. That nigga was no good.

"So, then what happened? Marcus tried to scare him off, didn't he?" I asked.

"No. Mega asked why I was on a date with a married man, and I'm like what? Marcus isn't married. But then, I looked down at his hand and sure enough, there was a ring on it."

My mouth dropped. "Ahh, bitch! I told you! Didn't I tell you that nigga had somebody else? I fuckin' knew it! A wife, though? A whole wife? But, he's telling you he doesn't want a relationship. I wish a nigga would—"

"Can I finish, please?"

"Yes," I nodded.

"Okay, so after that, I kinda went off on Marcus, and told him to leave. He did. Then, Mega told the girl he was with to leave and he came back at sat with me. We talked for a while, then I asked him to teach me how to shoot."

"Out of all the people to ask, you asked him? Why didn't you just ask Tristan?"

She rolled her eyes. "Because I didn't want Tristan to teach me. She shrugged and I gave her a look.

"Nah, you just wanted to hang out with Mega. You like him, don't you?"

Her eyes widened. "Like him? I barely know him. I just wanted him to—"

"Bitch, you're over there blushing! Look at you, liking a hood nigga. I never thought I'd see the day."

"I don't like him, Trinity. He's cool to talk to, but I'd never go further than that. I don't even want to see him again after what he made me do. He's crazy, for real."

"Girl," I laughed. "He didn't make you do anything you didn't wanna do. Don't blame that shit on him. Now, tell me about you killing someone. What happened? Did they try to kill you first?"

"No! Mega took me to this abandoned warehouse that's like a whole hour away from here, and he had someone tied up in there!"

"What?"

"Yeah, that's what I said, too. He gave me a gun and was like 'this is your first lesson'. He made me shoot that man that I didn't even know!"

I shook my head. "Don't blame that on him. He didn't force you to shoot that man. You chose to do it."

"Whatever," she said waving me off. "Either way, I shot him like three times, then I threw up. I've never seen anything like that up close before. I still can't believe I did it."

"I still can't believe you like Mega," I smirked at her.

"Would you stop saying that? I do not like that man. Don't go around telling people that, either."

"Bitch, who am I gonna tell? Tristan?"

"No, his brother. Maurice."

I twisted my face up. "Fuck that nigga. I don't even talk to him anymore." The thought of him pissed me off. Who the hell did he think he was? It had been a whole week, and I still hadn't heard from him. Stupid ass nigga.

"Really? I thought you two were gonna be something the way you were bragging about him and stuff. What happened?"

"Nothing," I said, flipping my hair. "He's just a stupid nigga and I don't have time for it."

Her phone started ringing next to her, and she rolled her eyes at it. "It's Tristan calling me again. I've been ignoring him for like a week."

"Why? Girl, answer the phone for that man. He probably thinks something happened to you."

"I just haven't been feeling like talking to him. This past week has been peaceful for me. There hasn't been any drama, I've been going to work and class like I was before my daddy died, and I feel like my normal self again. I know if I answer the phone for him, everything is just gonna get bad again."

"Answer the phone, Semaj. You probably got that nigga worried sick." I said, watching her blow out a breath.

She slid her finger across the screen, then put the phone on speaker. "Hello?"

"Semaj, what the fuck, yo? Why you ain't been answering the phone? Where the fuck you at?" he damn near yelled.

"I'm good, Tristan. I just needed to take a break from life. I needed time to think. Time to myself—"

"Man, fuck that shit! You got me out here thinking some terrible shit done happened to you! You could've sent me a text or some shit! I haven't been getting any sleep because I've been looking for your stupid ass!"

She rolled her eyes. "It's not that serious, Tristan. I just told you that I'm good. You don't know what I was going through, so you really have no right to yell at me like that. Obviously, you haven't been looking for me hard enough because—"

"Shut the fuck up, Semaj. Swear I'ma pop yo' ass in the mouth when I see you. I'm at ya dad's house on the Westside. Meet me there." He ended the call and she looked up at me.

"Don't look at me like that. You should've told him what was up. You got people gunning for you, now. You can't just be out here disappearing like that." I let her know.

"I'm grown. I can do what I want."

"Whatever, Semaj. You never listen to people when all they're trying to do is help you. You always make things difficult."

She smacked her lips. "But I needed a break. Everything in my life has taken a drastic turn. I'm not used to this."

"Yeah, I know, but the way you went about it was stupid. When you see Tristan, you need to apologize." I stood to my feet and grabbed my keys.

"Where the hell you about to go? You're leaving me?"

"I sure am. I got things to do today. I'll call you later, though." I blew her a kiss as I grabbed my purse and left.

I actually didn't have anything to do today. I didn't have to work, so I wanted to lay in my bed all day and watch movies.

As soon as I made it to my car, my phone was ringing. I rolled my eyes as I looked at the name popping up.

"The fuck this nigga want?" I muttered, hitting ignore. Two didn't wanna talk a week ago, so I don't know why he wants to talk now. Yeah, he did have some immaculate dick, but I wasn't about to be chasing his ass for it. I didn't know who the hell he thought I was.

It surprised me that he called right back. I smacked my lips and let it ring. He would get the message sooner or later that I didn't want to talk to him.

About fifteen minutes later, I was pulling up to my apartment building, eager to get back in my bed. I didn't get to do this often, so when I was able to, I got really excited about it. I already knew what movies I wanted to watch on Netflix, too. I made me a list the other day while I was at work.

"So, you didn't see me calling you?" I heard the familiar voice ask.

Are you fuckin' serious right now?

Two was leaning against my door with his arms folded. When I say this man was looking like a whole entire snack right now? I didn't know what it was, but he looked even better than he did when I first met his ass.

"What the hell you want, nigga?" I asked, folding my arms.

"I mean, I wanted you to answer your damn phone when I called."

"And I wanted you to call me back a week ago, but you didn't. So, now I don't wanna talk to you. Excuse me, I'm trying to get in my apartment."

"But I wanna talk to you," he tucked in his bottom lip.

"Bye, *Maurice*," I chuckled, gently pushing him out the way. "Get out the way, nigga."

"Nah, let's talk. Open the door, I don't want these nosey ass people all up in my business."

"No. I'm not letting you in. Go back to the hoe you was with all week. Leave me alone," As soon as the words left my lips, I regretted it. I sounded jealous of a nigga that wasn't even mine.

"Who said I was with a hoe last week, shawty? I was out here making this money." he said, and I waved him off.

"Whatever. I don't care. Now leave. It was good seeing you again." I gave him a small smile, then stuck my key in the door.

He pushed himself up against me causing a small gasp to leave my lips. "Open the door, shawty. I just wanna talk to you," he whispered against my ear, sending chills down my spine.

"No," I said. "I don't want you in here." My mouth was saying one thing, but my lady parts were saying another. I knew I needed to hurry up and get into my apartment because the more I was around him, the weaker I got.

"Open the door, Trinity." He demanded.

I sighed to myself as I unlocked the door, then pushed it open. I stepped in, and he stepped in right behind me and closed the door behind him.

I turned to glare at him. "Nigga, you said you wanted to talk, so talk. I don't got time for you—"

He smashed his lips against mine, and at this point, I didn't even fight it anymore. I was trying to play like I hadn't been thinking about having sex with this man, but we both knew the truth. He knew he had devil dick, and he knew how I felt about it.

"Stop talking that shit, girl." he said against my mouth. I felt his hand tugging at the rim of my pants, then, he slipped his hand in there. I let out a small moan once he let his fingers explore. "Shit drippin'," he chuckled, pulling his hand from in my pants, and putting his fingers— that were just inside of me, into his mouth.

I couldn't do anything but stare at him in awe. I ain't never had a nigga do anything like that.

"Uhh… I—"

"Just show me where the bedroom is, ma." he said lowly. He didn't have to tell me twice.

I quickly turned in the direction of my bedroom with him right on my heels. This isn't what I had planned to do today, but oh well. I deserved this. I deserved to get good dick at least once a month.

Once we were in the room, I hastily came out of my shirt and turned to watch him do the same. It took him a little minute to take his shirt off, but when he finally did it, I noticed the bandage wrapped around his shoulder.

"What happened to your shoulder?" I questioned.

"Got shot last week." he said, stepping out of his pants.

Suddenly, I felt bad. Here I was, mad at this man for not calling me back and he had been shot. He was having his own problems, and I was over here being jealous because I thought he was blowing me off for another bitch. I've got to do better.

I didn't say anything else as I came out the rest of my clothes, then waited for him to take over. My body was aching with anticipation. The last time we had sex, the shit was magical. I swear to God.

He slowly made his way over to me, then backed me up until I was sitting on the bed. Then, he got on his knees, spread my legs as far as they would go, and went to work with his tongue.

"Fuck," I groaned with my back arching and his arms locking down on my legs. The way his tongue slurped and licked had me ready to scream at the top of my lungs. Antonio's head never made me feel like this. I mean, it was alright, but it wasn't this.

"Keep these fuckin' legs open," he demanded, slapping the inside of my thigh. I nodded, but the job was easier said than done. The faster he licked, the more my legs shook, and the louder my moans got. I was trying to keep my legs open for him, but with every lick, they got closer and closer.

I could feel the orgasm rising, so I closed my eyes, ready to call out to the sex gods, but right before it happened, he pulled out. My eyes flew open as I looked at him.

"Two—"

"Shut the hell up." He lifted my body up off the edge of the bed and slowly slid into me, grabbing my hips to press into me even more. "Gahhh damn, this shit tight as fuck,"

He had his eyes closed as our bodies rocked together, but I couldn't keep my eyes off of him. Usually, I only went for the dark-skinned niggas, but Two won me over with his talk game. Then, on top of that, he was fine as hell.

He brought his body down on top of mine, and gently placed his lips on mine. He kissed me like he wasn't sure if he should do it or not... almost like he was scared to do it.

"Nah, nah, hold up," he said, snatching himself out of me. "Nah, shawty, turn around."

I guess I didn't move fast enough for him because he roughly flipped me on my stomach, then pulled me back to him by my hips. Once again, he slowly slid into me, causing my legs to get weak. He was delivering those slow, long strokes.

"Baby," I sighed as trailed his hand up my spin until he reached my neck, then finally my hair. He wasted no time tangling his fingers in my hair, then pulling it. "Shitttt."

He yanked my head back so that I was straight up on my knees. He gently placed kisses on my neck and shoulders, all while still giving me those deadly strokes.

"This shit mine, aight?" he hissed, as he brought his other hand to the front of my body and caressed my breast. He found the nipple and tugged at it, and I trembled in his arms. "Aight?"

Honestly, I didn't even remember what he'd just said to me. I felt like I couldn't even hear anymore. So, I chose to act like I didn't hear his ass.

So, by the time we were actually done with each other, we laid in my bed, bodies sore, but sore with pleasure. He couldn't keep his hands off of me. He was rubbing, caressing, and at one point, he even held my foot in his hands and massaged it. This was something I wasn't expecting from him. I just thought hood niggas were always tough and didn't know how to be affectionate.

"You didn't even come over here to talk," I said, gently running my hand up his chest.

"I did," he nodded. "I said all I needed to say with my dick. That nigga always know what to say."

"Boy bye. You annoying as fuck." I laughed.

"But my dick ain't."

"I mean, you got 'aight' dick. You don't got that—"

"Bullshit," he chuckled. "Shit had you climbing the walls and shit. Don't try to downplay my shit."

I smiled at him. I wonder how old he was when he found out he had good dick. He's probably had bitches chasing him his entire life.

"Like I said, it was aight." I said watching him throw the covers off the both of us.

"Bet. Let's go again, then."

ALAYA

"Mmmm, haven't seen a nigga that fine in a while," I said to myself as I watched the light-skinned nigga move across the parking lot and into the corner store. I had no business being on this side of town, but this was how I found my money.

I looked at myself in the mirror, then quickly got out the car. Let's see how long it would take this nigga to give me his number. Usually, on this side of town, it never took long.

I flipped my hair as I pulled the door open, then let my eyes scan the small as store. There was a crackhead in there yelling, but everyone around here was used to that shit. I think her name was Betty. She'd always be somewhere begging, then popping off at the mouth when someone told her they weren't giving her ass any money.

"Fuck y'all broke ass bitches!" she yelled, as I looked at her. Bitch looked disgusting. She had on a long white, dingy shirt that was full of holes, she couldn't fit her jeans, so she was holding them up with one hand, her hair was thrown all over the place, and I swear she had like two teeth. It was sad to see people out here looking like this. Sad as fuck.

"Betty, take yo' ass on, man. You know they gon' call the cops on yo' ass again," I heard a voice say to her. Once I matched the voice with a face, I smiled. He was even finer up close.

I grabbed a bag of chips and made it my business to walk in front of him. I could feel his eyes on me as I sat my bag of chips on the counter to pay for them. It was getting harder and harder to contain my smile.

You know when you look good, you feel even better. I felt like I was walking on a cloud right now. I was wearing an olive-green dress that hugged my body and showed off my damn near perfect figure. I had my toes out because they had just got a new paint job, and my jet-black weave was flowing down my back, stopping right above my ass.

"Thank you," I said to the man behind the register after I paid for my chips. I gave the fine light bright nigga one last look before I left out of the store completely.

This nigga should be following behind me in three... two... one...

"Ayo, ma!" I heard from behind me.

I smiled to myself as I turned to look at him. He was doing a light jog to catch up with me.

"Can I help you?" I asked, with a brow lifted.

"Nah, I'm good," he said, causing me to look at him like he was crazy. "But, I just wanted to let you know that your dress is stuck in your panties, shawty."

Bruhhh.

I looked to see if he was telling the truth, and sure enough, my dress was stuck in my thong, causing instant embarrassment.

"Oh," I said, voice full of defeat. "Well, thank you..." I pulled my dress from my underwear and watched as he smiled at me.

"No problem. You gotta be more careful when you leave the bathroom. Ain't no telling how many niggas saw ya ass cheeks today."

He was making me feel worse about it. I was actually wishing he would walk the fuck off. I didn't even want his number anymore.

"I said thanks," I let out, turning to make my way to my car.

"Aye wait," he held, catching up with me again. "What's your name? You from here? I ain't never saw yo' ass before."

"Alaya. Yeah, I'm from here. Born and raised in the A, baby. Now if you'll excuse me, I got somewhere to be—"

"Put your number in my phone first. We should definitely link one day."

I fought the urge to smile again. I was out here looking like a dumb bitch, and he was still trying to get my number.

"No thank you," I declined. "I don't give my number out to strangers. I don't even know your name."

"Tristan," he smiled. Nigga's teeth were straight as hell. Then those lips? It was hard as hell acting like I wasn't interested in this man.

"Well, Tristan, you're still a stranger so—"

"So, give me your number so I can change that. I think I deserve it... I mean, I did just help yo' ass out unlike the rest of these niggas that was probably just staring at yo' ass and shit."

I bit down on my bottom lip as I tried to think of something to say back to him. What if I gave this man my number and he didn't even use it?

"Fine," I finally said, sticking my hand out for the phone.

He gave it to me and smiled the entire time I keyed my number in.

"Lay," he said, reading the contact out loud. "When I call you, you better answer."

I playfully rolled my eyes. "Okay, Tristan. I'll be sure to answer." I didn't wait for a response from him as I turned to get in my car.

Mission fuckin' accomplished.

Now, I was just hoping this nigga didn't disappoint me. Whenever I met a fine ass dude, I would always have my hopes up about the sex. I'd be daydreaming about the shit, only to get my feelings hurt because the dick would be trash. It always happened. But, if I fucked with an ugly nigga? He would always give me the best dick of my life. Shit was crazy.

As I pulled up to a red light, my phone rang in my lap, and I quickly answered it.

"Hey boo," I said into the phone.

"What the fuck, Alaya?!" my sister, Lauren, snapped. "You know you're all over the internet right now?"

"Damn, for real? What am I doing?"

"You're getting fucked at a damn party! You're letting this nigga fuck you in front of hella people! I thought I told you to chill out, bruh! Why you always out here doing stupid shit?"

I rolled my eyes. "Man, it's really not even that serious, Lauren. What you so mad about?"

"Not that serious?! Alaya, your ass and titties is all over the internet! You're going viral right now! This is serious!"

"But, it's really not." I didn't even remember last night, honestly. I remember going to a party, I remember popping a pill with this nigga I met, I remember getting hella drunk, but after that? I didn't remember a damn thing.

"Where you at? You at home?"

"Nope. I'm driving, looking for a new nigga. I don't know what time I'll be home today." I let her know. I actually was going home, I just didn't want her to come over and give me even more lectures. I was good. I was living life. Why was she so worried about me?

"Man," she sighed. "Just call me when you get home. We really need to talk."

Bitch, there ain't shit to talk about. Always being so damn dramatic.

"Okay, Lauren. I'll let you know when I get there. Oh, and send me that video, please. I wanna see it." I ended the call, knowing that would piss her off, but I didn't care. Nothing could dampen the mood I was in right now.

It took me a little over twenty minutes to get back home, and as soon as I pulled into my driveway, my phone was vibrating with a text message from my sister.

"Took her ass long enough," I muttered, as I opened the video to watch it.

The video started with me and some white dude. I was giving him head, and yeah, there were hella people around. I skipped a few minutes into the video, and we were fucking on the kitchen table while everyone around cheered and had their phones out.

"My hair looks a fuckin' mess," I scoffed as I fast forwarded to the end of the video where he came all over my face. I didn't remember any of this happening. It looked like I had the time of my life last night, though.

I was trying to watch the video over again, but my phone started ringing in my hand. It was an unknown number, and I almost ignored it, but it could've been important.

"Hello?" I said, popping the door open, and stepping out the car.

"What's up? I thought you'd gave me the wrong number or something."

"Tristan? Damn, I didn't expect you to call so soon." I walked to the mail box and pulled the mail from it, then headed towards the front door.

"I wasn't doing shit, so I thought I'd call you. No need to waste time thinking about doing it when I can actually do the shit."

I nodded like he could see me. "True shit. What you got going on, though? You don't work?" I unlocked the door, then pushed it open.

"Yeah, I work. I work on my own time, though."

"Mmmm," I said, flipping through the mail. Nothing but bills. I wish someone would be nice and send me a fucking check or something.

WHAP!

My phone flew out of my hand as I felt the stinging on my face. I looked up seeing Dez standing over me looking like a mad man.

"Nigga, you done lost your got damn mind or something?!" I snapped, picking my phone up off the floor. "How the fuck you even get in my house to begin with?!"

"Bitch, how the fuck you think I got in here?! Where the fuck you been at?! Why am I seeing your hoe ass sucking dick all over the internet?!" he boomed. To any other woman, his loud ass voice probably would've scared them, but nothing about Dez scared me. I went toe to toe with this nigga all the time.

"You good?" Tristan asked. I could hear the concern in his voice.

"Yeah, I'm good. I just got an intruder in my house and shit." I walked away from Dez.

"What? Where you at? You need me to come—"

"Who the fuck you on the phone with, Alaya?! You walking away from me like I'm not talking to you and shit?! You got me fucked up, yo!" Dez hollered.

"Nah, I'm good," I let Tristan know. "Bitch, get the fuck out my house! Why the fuck you even in here?! I'm about to call the police on your stupid ass!"

"You need to call me back? I can—"

"You gon' call who?" Dez asked, pulling me by my hair.

Alright. Now, this nigga was doing the fucking most.

"Hold on, Tristan." I said, tossing the phone to the floor, then squaring up with Dez. "What's up, nigga? You wanna fight? Let's fuckin' do it!"

I swung at him, catching him in his mouth, then sent two more, causing him to stumble. This isn't what I had planned to do when I got home today. I couldn't believe this nigga was really in my house like this!

"Chill the fuck out, Alaya!" he yelled, wiping his mouth.

"Nah! Why you here? Get the hell out!" I swung at him again, but he dodged it. I guess he was getting tired of me swinging because he grabbed me by my neck and pinned me against the wall.

He quickly pulled his gun from the waist of his pants and pressed it into my temple.

"You know I'll body yo' ass right here, Alaya! Why the fuck you playing with me?!"

"Then do it, nigga! You a pussy, anyway! I don't give a fuck about you! I never gave a fuck about you, Dez!" He hit me in the nose with his gun, then released me. I fell to the floor and looked up at him.

Dez was ugly. He was fat, too, but he had money. That was the only reason I gave him the time of day, anyway. I would never be seen in public with that clown. On top of all that, he was a coke head. He was probably acting crazy right now because he was high off that shit.

"Where the fuck were you last night, bruh?" he asked, kneeling down in front of me.

"Why does it matter? You're not my nigga, you've never been my nigga, and you'll never be my nigga. Get the fuck out of my house. I'm not gonna say it again,"

I stood to my feet and walked away from him. That's when I realized Tristan was still on the phone, and he probably heard everything that just happened between me and Dez.

I picked the phone up and put it to my ear. "Hello?"

"Yeah... you good?"

I let out a breath. "Yeah, I'm good. Niggas just stupid." I flipped my hair from my face and sat down on the couch. Dez came to sit next to me and I sighed loudly. "You know what, I'm gonna call you back."

"Aight." I ended the call for real this time, then glared at Dez.

"I know I told you to leave, nigga. What the fuck are you still sitting here for?" I spat.

He rubbed his nose and looked at me. "Why you do that? Why you act like you don't give a fuck about anything or anybody?"

I let out a laugh. "Who the fuck said I'm acting?"

"Man, I'm out here tellin' niggas me and you rockin' and you out here fucking niggas at parties and shit? Man, you didn't even care that you were being recorded." He pulled a hand down his face and I rolled my eyes.

"First of all, why the fuck you out there telling people we're together? We barely fuck, now. We have nothing going on. Why the hell you acting so sprung for?"

"Mannnn," he sighed. "I ain't never acted like this over no bitch." I wiped my nose with my hand. This nigga really hit me in the face with his damn gun. This right here is why I won't fuck with him. He's too fuckin' comfortable putting his hands on women, and what the hell I look like being with a coke head?

"I really don't know why you're acting like this over me. We both know that I'm not shit. Don't know how yo' goofy ass caught feelings and shit." I stood to my feet, then moved towards the bathroom. This nigga really had my nose leaking.

When I got inside the bathroom, I saw that I had a busted lip, too. I smacked my lips as I gathered the tissue for my nose. I was ready for his ass to leave. We didn't have anything to talk about, so he really didn't have a reason to be here.

"Bye, Dez," I said, walking out of the bathroom.

He looked up at me and shook his head. "Nah, lemme chill over here for a little bit. You know you don't got shit to do today." he said.

"You don't know what I have planned to do, nigga! Just leave. Don't make me call my brothers over here. I know you don't wanna deal with them again."

He sighed. "Come on, Alaya. Don't do me like that."

Dez knew he didn't wanna deal with my brothers, Chris, Shiloh, and Karter. This one time, Dez came over drunk one night, trying to fight and shit. I was high as hell off weed and pills, and here he comes to fuck up my night. Long story short, he punched me in the face like I was a nigga, I called my brothers, and they came over here and beat the hell out of that nigga.

Dez didn't talk to me for a while after that, but that didn't really last long. I couldn't understand why he wanted me so bad. We weren't even having sex anymore.

"Bye, Dez." I said. I'm sure he could hear the annoyance in my voice. This nigga was acting like he was deaf or some shit.

"Whatever yo," he said, standing to his feet. "I'll call you later. Answer my shit, too."

I rolled my eyes and watched him walk out the door.

"I'm not answering shit from your stupid ass." I muttered, then went to lock the door. I couldn't stand a nigga that couldn't take no for an answer. That shit was so annoying. "Can't fuckin' stand niggas, period."

SEMAJ

"Nah, for real, I thought somebody had found yo' ass and had you tied up somewhere," Antonio said, as I rolled my eyes.

"Yeah, for real, that was some real stupid shit you did."

"Okay, but I'm here. I don't really see what the big deal is." I said as I sat down on the couch. I was slowly coming to terms with everything. I looked at my bank account today, and almost passed out. I've never even read a number that big before, let alone in my damn bank account.

"Man, just don't do this shit again, Semaj. You need to let me know where you're at, at all times. You never know what might happen."

"Okay, Tristan." I sighed, I felt like I was a child with overly strict parents. It was definitely going to take some time getting used to this.

"You own businesses now. You need to check in at least once a week. Make sure everything is running smoothly." he went on. I swear, if I rolled my eyes one more time, they would get stuck.

I folded my arms. "Anything else, *dad?*" I asked, sarcastically.

"Man, you need to take this shit serious, Semaj."

"I am taking it serious. Who wouldn't take people trying to kill them serious?" Before Tristan could respond, my phone was vibrating in my purse. I quickly pulled it out, only to see a text from Mega.

Mega: U Busy tonight?

I suppressed a smile. I hadn't really talked to Mega since last week because he's freakin' crazy, but him sending me a text had me feeling like I'd just gotten a text from my high school crush.

Me: I might be. Why?

I knew for a fact I wasn't busy tonight. Well, unless Tristan has something planned for me, but I highly doubt that.

Mega: Come through tonight. I wanna see u.

This time, I couldn't suppress the smile. He wanted to see lil ole me? I'm not gonna lie and say I haven't been thinking about him. I would just be sitting on the couch, watching TV, then I would find myself thinking about him.

I thought about what sex would be like with him. Yeah, I know I said he wasn't my type, but that was something that I couldn't get from my mind. I even dreamed about it, one night. It was crazy.

"You not even listening, yo. You too busy smiling at your phone and shit." Tristan snapped, causing me to look up at him.

"Tristan, hush. You've been smiling at your phone since I've got here. Don't come for me." I said, replying to Mega's message.

Me: Address?

A part of me was afraid to see him again, but the other part of me was almost too eager to get back in his presence again.

"You need to make sure you always got a strap on you," Antonio said.

"You need to make sure you know how to use the strap, too. It would be pointless to just walk around with the shit if you're not gonna pull that mothafucka out and blast it." Tristan chimed in.

"I was actually fine this past week. I wasn't in danger at all. I think I can take care of myself pretty well," I let them know.

They both laughed like I had told the funniest joke. I didn't understand what the hell was so funny.

"That just means you got lucky, Semaj. You need to listen to what the fuck me and Antonio are telling you. We're like the only family you have left."

"Thanks for reminding me," I murmured. "Can we do this tomorrow? I actually have somewhere to be tonight."

"Yeah, I got some shit of my own to get into, too." Antonio said, gathering his things from the kitchen table. "I'll holla at y'all niggas later,"

I'm not a nigga, dick head.

Antonio walked out of the house and I looked at Tristan. "I'll see you later. I'll make sure to call and check in with you since I'm a child," I said, making my way towards the door.

"I'm just trying to keep you safe, Semaj." he said, pulling a hand down his face. I didn't respond to him as I left from the house.

Once I was outside, I unlocked my car, and got in it. I forgot to mention that I'd brought me a new car last week. A 2016 Mercedes Benz, actually. I also went shopping and bought me a new wardrobe since all my things got burned when they decided to catch my house on fire.

Living in one of my dad's old houses was a little weird. I mean, I was beyond grateful that he had so many houses around, but I still wanted my own. I had enough money to buy my own place, so that's what I planned on doing. I just got a weird vibe like someone was watching me in my dad's house. It made me feel eerie.

About twenty minutes later, I was pulling into the driveway, and the nerves were setting in. I'd never been to Mega's house, so I didn't know what to expect. How should I dress? Sexy? Or, should I just keep it casual? I wanted to text him and ask, but I decided against it. I'm sure I had something in my closet that would work.

It seemed like I couldn't get the door unlocked fast enough, but when I did, I hurried up the stairs and into my room. I took longer than I usually would in the shower because I made sure to shave everything. I wasn't going to go over there throwing it at him, but if he wanted to have sex, I definitely wasn't going to turn it down.

After my extra-long shower, I wrapped my oversized towel around my body and made my way to the closet. Almost everything hanging in my closet still had the tags on it.

I thought about wearing a dress, but when I tried it on, I felt like I was trying too hard.

"Why did I even waste money on this?" I sighed, looking at myself in the full-length mirror.

It was a tan dress that stopped in the middle of my thighs and hugged my body. It did a little bit too much, if you asked me. It made my booty look like the ones these women are out here paying for. Yeah, I had sex on the mind, but I didn't want Mega to feel like that's the only reason I was coming over.

I opted for some nude flare out pants, and a white tank top. Casual, but cute. The pants didn't hug my body like the dress did, so I felt a lot better in these.

After I was finished with my outfit, I quickly ran my brush through my hair, and sprayed a little perfume on myself. Not too much, but just enough.

I slid my black pumps on my feet, then I was out the door and in my car. As I searched through my phone for Mega's address, nerviness washed over me. I didn't know why, all of a sudden, I was afraid to be in the same place as Mega.

The feeling got worse when my GPS said Mega's house was only ten minutes away from where I was at.

"Goodness," I said, backing out of the driveway. "Of course, he lives close to me." I could feel my heart drumming against my chest. I had a right mind to tell him that something came up, and I couldn't make it to his place, but I didn't. I had spent way too much time getting ready for this.

Pulling into his driveway, I was amazed at how big his house was. What did he do for a living again? I don't believe he told me. Either way, he was making money. His house looked like something straight out of a magazine. I couldn't wait to see what the inside looked like.

I checked my appearance in the mirror before stepping out of the car. It seemed like it took me forever to get to his front door, but when I finally made it, I lifted my hand to knock, then waited patiently for him to answer it.

I took a couple of deep breaths, trying to calm myself down, but I could already feel my palms sweating. The last time I felt like this was the first day of college. Everything about college used to make me nervous. Now, everything about Mega was making me nervous.

The door finally swung open, and Mega stood there shirtless, only wearing a pair of sweats, and a blunt was hanging from him lips.

"Oh damn, shawty, why didn't you let a nigga know you were on the way?" he asked, stepping to the side so I could step in.

"I'm sorry. I didn't think about it." He closed the door, then lead the way to the living room.

Just as I suspected, the inside of the house looked even better. I could tell a man lived here, just like at Tristan's house. The stripper pole in the middle of the living room didn't surprise me, either.

I gave him a sly look as he eyed my entire body like a piece of meat.

"You don't know nothing about that," he said, as I sat down on the couch. "You want some brownies? I just made them bitches,"

"Actually, I would love some brownies." He smiled at me, then made his way into the kitchen, quickly returning with a pan of brownies in his hand.

"They hot as fuck," he let me know, sitting the pan on the table in front of me. "Help yourself, though."

"Look at you, cooking for me. That's so nice of you, Mega." I took a brownie from the pan and took a bite out of it. I didn't want to sound dramatic or anything, but that was one of the best things I ever tasted.

"Yeah, my shits legendary, ain't they? I could go into business selling these."

His hair was in two braids today. I think I liked him the best with this hairstyle. I don't know, he looked... cleaner than he usually did. Was that the word I was looking for? No, it wasn't. This man looked good.

Delicious.

Immaculate.

He looked like the type of man to hold the door open for me, then slap my ass as I walked past.

"Or, you could just keep making them for me," I smiled, watching him get relaxed on the couch. I was trying to keep my eyes on the top of his body, but with the sweat pants he was wearing, I could see his dick print perfectly. I could see the outline, which made my mouth water. I wonder what he would do if I put my hand in his—

"I didn't even think yo' little ass was gonna come over here. After I sent my address and you didn't text back, I low key got pissed off."

I didn't know what was going on with me. The only thing I had on my mind was sex. I wanted to skip the small talk and have sex with him in every room of this house.

"Why would you think that? It's not like you're crazy or anything or have me in warehouses shooting innocent people I don't know," I let out, sarcastically.

"Semmy, that nigga wasn't innocent. You ever stop to think why I would have an innocent mothafucka locked up in a warehouse?"

I rolled my eyes. "No, but I didn't know him. therefore, he was innocent. He didn't do anything to me, and I killed him. Remind me not to ask you to teach me how to do anything else, okay?"

"Damn, I thought I was a pretty good teacher. You hurting my feelings, Semmy."

"So, you're really gonna call me that? You really just gave me a whole new name?"

He chuckled lightly. "You call me Mega, and I don't be complaining to you about that shit."

"Because that's your name!"

"And Semmy is your name," he shrugged, easily.

"Whatever," I said, letting him have it. Clearly, this man was going to call me whatever the hell he wanted to.

"How you feeling, though? You good?" His questions caught me off guard, and I don't even know why. I guess I thought he was the type of man who didn't care about my feelings, like Marcus.

"I'm good," I said. "Good as I can be. I still wish I could go back to my old life, but there's nothing I can do about that now."

"My pops died the day I was born. Never even got to meet the nigga."

"That's terrible. I'm so sorry to hear that. So, you and Maurice had different dads?"

He gave me a look before he let out a small laugh. "Yo, I gotta get used to your proper ass using people's real names and shit. But yeah, we got different dads."

"Y'all look nothing alike," I said, thinking back to the one time I'd seen his brother.

"Yeah, I know. I look way better." It was the truth, but I wasn't going to say that. It was tasteless.

I glanced over at the pole that was in the middle of the floor and I couldn't help to think about the type of mess Mega has going on in here. I mean, there was nothing wrong with having the stripper pole, but why put it in the living room? Out of all the rooms in the house, this is the one he decided?

"You keep looking at that shit like you wanna do something," he said causing me to give him a small smirk.

"No thank you."

"Nah, I'm just playing with yo ass. You probably wouldn't know what to do on it, anyway."

I lifted a brow as I looked at him. I always liked a challenge.

"What are you saying? That I can't pole dance?"

He nodded. "That's exactly what I'm saying, shawty. Nothing on you, though. You—"

"Let's see, then." I said, flipping my hair and standing to my feet. "Play some music."

At first, he looked at me like I was crazy. He probably thought that I was playing, but I was serious.

I stood in front of the pole and examined it. Then, I slipped my shoes off, and did the same with my pants and watched as his eyes lustfully roamed all over my body. I was so glad that I decided to wear a cute thong today instead of granny panties.

He tapped away at his phone and moments later, Privacy by Chris Brown started playing through the speakers.

"I need your body in wayyyyy, that you don't understand but I'm losing my patience..."

Once I heard his voice fill the room, I kicked my shoes out the way, ready to grab the pole, but Mega stopped me.

"Nah, Nah, put them bitches back on." He said, referring to my shoes. He was sitting all the way up on the couch, ready for what I was about to do.

I smiled to myself as I put my shoes back on.

"Girl I just wanna take you home, and right to it..."

As the best dropped, I seductively walked around the pole, with my eyes never leaving his.

"Know I gotta kiss it baby, give it to me, lick it, lick it, inside and out..."

I stopped walking and started climbing the pole. Once I felt like I was high enough, I released my legs, tightened my abs, then flipped upside down, slowly sliding down the pole with my legs spreading apart. Once I got up from the floor, I climbed up the pole again, but this time, I extended my legs, let the pole go and let my back arch.

I was feeling good. I didn't know what this feeling was that I'd never felt before, but it honestly felt like I was floating. I glanced at Mega and he was looking like he was ready to cum on himself.

Did I mention that I take a pole dancing class once a week? No, I didn't want to be a stripper whatsoever, but pole dancing was great fitness. That was how I stayed in shape.

As Chris Brown sang, I did flips and tricks until Mega finally stood up and made his way over to me. He stood in front of me, faces just inches apart, not saying a word.

"Why do I feel like this?" I asked, more to myself. "Why do I feel—"

"Because that brownie you ate had weed in it,"

My mouth fell open. Was he serious? He really let me eat that brownie and didn't feel the need to let me know what was in it? How dare him?

"Mega—"

He grabbed my face, then stuck his tongue down my throat. Everything I was about to say to him flew right out the window. The only thing I could focus on was his mouth being on mine.

"You making my dick hard," he muttered against my lips. Before I could even think about a response, he scooped me up, bridal style, and carried me up the stairs. I wanted to get a small tour of his house as we walked, but I couldn't. I was too busy kissing all over his neck, ready to give him my body.

When we finally made it to his big ass room, he closed the door behind him with his foot, then locked it, like there were other people in the house or something. He gently laid me on the bed, then I quickly took my shirt off. I didn't have time to be waiting on him to take off my clothes. I could do it myself.

I tugged at the rim of his pants, letting him know that I was ready. What the hell was he just standing there for?

He slapped my hand away and smiled. "I got it, shawty. I'm a grown ass man."

I fought the urge to roll my eyes. "Well hurry your grown ass up, Mega."

He licked his lips. "Beg for it."

My brows came together as I twisted my mouth. Why was he playing with me? I'm not begging to have sex with him. Why did I have to beg when we both wanted it?

I folded my arms and looked at him. "Mega—"

"I was joking shawty, chill." He quickly came out of his sweats, then his boxers, then walked over to the light to turn it off.

It was dark, but I could still see his dick swinging, and my mouth went dry. Marcus was a decent size, but he didn't have anything on Mega. Mega's actually had me wanting to change my mind about everything and go home.

Once he pulled me by my foot and spread my legs, I knew there was no turning back now.

He started with kissing this inside of my thighs. I could hear my heart drumming in my ears, but there was no way I was going to tell him I was scared. Honestly, he probably knew. He could probably see it all over my face.

His kissed moved lower and lower, and every time his lips touched my skin, I would feel the chills running down my spine. Once he was done kissing all over my legs, he came back to kiss the spot that actually counts. I know, I probably shouldn't compare Marcus and Mega, but my goodness. Mega was just better than him in every single way.

He put my legs back as far as they would go, then dove in.

"Shit," I moaned, feeling his tongue swirl all around my womanhood. Instantly, my legs started shaking. Wait, no. My entire body was shaking and he hadn't even been at it for five minutes. The more he licked, the harder it was for my legs to stay where they were.

In one swift motion, he came up for air, and next thing I knew, he was slowly entering me.

"Wait," I breathed, trying to push him away.

"Nah. Chill, shawty," he grunted. "Relax. Why you so tense?"

"Because it hurts! Go slow!"

He chuckled and looked at me. "I am going slow. You just gotta relax. I'm not gonna hurt you."

Bullshit. He wasn't even all the way in, and it was hurting. I never felt this much pain while having sex with someone else. I don't think I even felt this much pain when I lost my virginity.

He started kissing all over my neck, then slowly moved to chin, then my lips. I felt him sliding into me again and I squeezed my eyes shut.

"Fuck," he muttered, still going slow. At this point, I was ready for it to be over. The more he went, the more it hurt. "You gotta relax, Semaj."

I shook my head with my eyes still closed tight. "No,"

"Look at me,"

I opened my eyes and looked straight into his. Did I mention they were light brown? I think there was something new that I found I liked about him every time I saw him.

While I was too busy falling in love with his eyes, he slid himself all the way inside me, causing a light gasp to escape my throat. For a moment, I was paralyzed. I couldn't do anything but dig my nails into his skin.

"Shit," he hissed, then quickly pulled out of me. "Nah, you virgin tight." He let me know while slapping my vagina with his penis. Without warning, he entered me again, and I could feel tingling all over my body.

"Wait!" I groaned, trying to get away from him, but he wouldn't let me.

"Nah, ma. Take this dick."

I'm not trying to be dramatic or anything, but I swear I could feel this man's penis hitting the back of my vagina. Was this normal? Why were my toes tingling like this? Does he have sex with everyone like this?

He leaned up to watch himself go in and out, and I thought I was gonna lose it. I could feel the climax coming.

"Megaaa!" I'm sure he could feel me about to release because I was squeezing the hell out of him with my legs.

"Fuck girl," he pulled out again and dove back in with his tongue.

"Mmmm, babyyyy,"

"Turn that ass around." he demanded in a low, husky voice.

I did what he said with no questions asked. I smiled to myself as I put my face in the pillow and ass in the air. I don't even remember the last time I had done this position.

This time, he didn't go slow. Nope. He plunged right in, making me yell out in pleasure. I thought I was gonna keep my head in the pillow, but he had other plans. He grabbed me by my neck and pulled my body to his.

"Oh my God, Mega!" I shrieked, feeling him pound into me. He was moaning softly in my ear, making everything so much better.

"Yeah baby. Say my mothafuckin' name."

"Meg—"

"Nah, tell me you love me, shawty."

"Huh?"

"You fuckin' heard me."

"I love you, Mega!"

He tightened his grip around my neck just as I released all over him.

"Ahhh, fuckkkk!"

He collapsed on top of me, and I was all smiles. Sex with him was everything I imagined it to be.

"You tryna get married tomorrow?" he asked, breathing heavy.

I giggled. "Shut up, Mega."

14

ALAYA

"I just don't understand how you're okay with this, Alaya. Everyone is seeing you naked all over the internet." Lauren said as I rolled my eyes. She really came all the way to my house just to run her mouth about what I do with my life. She really needs to get her some business to worry about.

"Girl, I used to be a whole stripper. How's that any different?"

"Because you weren't having sex! Taking off your clothes for money is one thing, but fucking? While people watch? Do you have any morals?"

I didn't say anything as I licked the blunt to seal it. Her favorite thing to say about me was I didn't have any morals. She always told me that I wasn't going to find a husband because of it. Little did she know, I didn't give not one fuck about finding a damn husband. Who the hell said I wanted to be married, anyway?

"Do you have anything to do other than worrying about my life? I feel like we have this conversation at least once a week, and I'm honestly tired of it." I let her know, looking around my living room for a lighter.

I know I got a lighter somewhere around here.

"Alaya, I only say something about it because I care! What kind of sister would I be if I didn't say anything about it?"

"A sister that minds her own damn business. You know, I'd actually prefer if you did mind your business. You'd probably be much happier." I finally found the lighter that I was sitting on, and I lit my blunt. This smoke session would be even better if Lauren would take her ass home or something.

"You're going down a dangerous path, though. I don't understand how you're not seeing it. You don't care about anything!"

I chuckled, lightly. "I care about making money."

"That's it? You don't care about your family? Or, how bad you're making us all look? What if Chris saw this video? Then what?" she asked, as I inhaled the smoke. She was so funny to me.

Lauren was the sibling that couldn't wait to tell on you. She prided herself on being the favorite, so she did whatever she had to do maintain that, including making her other siblings look bad. With that being said, I already knew she'd told the entire family about the video, and probably showed them too. That's why I was having trouble understanding why she was over here.

"Stop playing, Lauren," I laughed. "You know you've already told the entire family."

"What? I have not. I don't wanna see the look on mom's face when she finds out her youngest daughter is out here having sex at parties. I can't believe you, Alaya. You were raised better than that."

"Okay," I said, standing to my feet. "It's time for you to go. Thank you for stopping by and trying to lecture me once again, but I'm good. It's my life, and I'll be damned if I listen to mothafuckas trying to tell me how to live it. You're my sister, and I love you, but you got me fucked up. Get the hell out."

I knew she was shocked by what I'd just said to her by the look on her face, but I really didn't care.

"Wow, Alaya. I can't believe you." she said, standing to her feet. She flipped her hair off her shoulder and made her way to the door. "I think you should come to church with us this Sunday. Mom would love to see you—"

"You must be out of your damn mind if you think I'm about to go to that church with all those fake ass people. Nah, I'm not going. Don't even get your hopes up."

She stood there looking at me for a while, before she shook her head and walked out the door. I let out a sigh of relief once she was gone. Out of all of my siblings, she was my least favorite. My brothers minded their business. Lauren made sure to put herself in your business. I swear, it was the most annoying thing ever.

I sat back down on the couch and found something to watch on TV. Now that my annoying ass sister was gone, I could get back to relaxing.

"Fuck," I sighed. "I'm hungry as hell."

I thought about just ordering pizza, but I'd been eating pizza all damn week. Honestly, I didn't want fast food, either. It was a Friday night in Atlanta, so I knew wherever I went, I would have to wait in line regardless.

I blew out a breath as I got up from the couch. Soul food was sounding really good right now. The only thing was, I wished they delivered. I didn't wanna leave my house, but there wasn't shit in here to cook. Fuck I look like cooking anyway?

I put my blunt out to save it until I got back, then I was on my way out the door. It probably took me a good ten minutes to get to the restaurant, and once I saw how many people were in the parking lot, I started regretting even leaving my house.

"I should've just fuckin' ordered pizza again," I muttered as I drove around the parking lot for the third time. I didn't wanna park far as hell from the place, but that was the only way I was going to be able to park at all.

I blew out a breath as I parked my car, then I checked myself in the mirror. I ran my fingers through my weave, then quickly hopped out the car. I wanted this to be quick, but I knew I'd probably have to wait. This shit was crazy. Why everybody wanna eat here tonight? They needed to go home and cook, shit.

"Man, nah, Trinity won't even talk to my ass anymore," I heard a nigga say. He was talking loud as hell.

"Nigga, I been told you to stop cheating on her, but you don't listen to nobody. She probably found somebody else to occupy her time with." His friend replied. I smiled to myself because the voice was familiar. Shit, too familiar.

I hadn't talked to Tristan since the other day. Honestly, I hadn't been thinking about him enough to call him, and clearly, he hadn't been thinking about me either because I hadn't heard from his ass. This was a perfect opportunity to talk to him.

I flipped my hair from my shoulder as I approached him. The smile on my face was from ear to ear, but I quickly wiped it off once I was all up in his personal space.

"So, you think you can just give me good dick like that, then act like I don't exist?" I asked, folding my arms and watching him look at me with wide eyes.

"Yo, shorty, what you—"

"That's real fucked up, Tristan. I've been thinking about that dick all day and night, and you out here ignoring me? Like I didn't mean shit to you? Nigga, you know my head is immaculate. You ain't shit!"

"Chill out, bruh. I ain't never stuck my dick inside you—"

"So, we're lying now? You wasn't saying shit like that when you had your tongue all in my ass! You had my shits spread all the way open!" I hollered, pretending like I was spreading something with my hands.

His friend let out a small chuckle. "Damn, Tristan. That's why you be having these bitches going crazy, because you out here eating booty."

"Man, I ain't out here eating ass! The fuck you even talking about?" he glared at me and I gave him a small smile.

"No need to lie, my nigga. You good at the shit. The way you kiss both ass cheeks before you spread them? Shit was legendary." His friend twisted his face up and was giving him the 'you eat ass nigga?' look. It was getting harder and harder for me to contain my laughter.

"Look, shawty. I don't even know your name." Tristan said, which caused me to raise a brow. He knew my name. He was just embarrassed.

"Yes, you do. You were moaning it like a little bitch when I had ya balls in my mouth," I glanced at his friend. "Does he always lie like this?"

His friend shrugged and Tristan glared at him. I let out a small chuckle and flipped my hair.

"Well, whenever you feel like licking between my ass cheeks again, call me. You have my number," I walked away before he could even respond. By the time I got into the restaurant, I was laughing hysterically. People were looking at me like I was crazy, and I didn't even care. I knew either Tristan would be calling me soon or he'd come in here to talk to me.

The line was ridiculous. If I wasn't this hungry, I definitely wouldn't be standing here right now. The shit I do for food.

"Aye," I heard from behind me. I didn't turn around, though. I was gonna act like I didn't even hear his ass. "Yo, you really that crazy, or you was just tryna be funny?" Tristan asked, standing directly behind me. He was so close, I could feel the heat radiating from his body.

"Don't know what you're talkin' about," I said, still facing forward. I knew he was gonna come talk to me, but I didn't know that it was going to be right now.

"Man, don't do that shit. And look at me when I'm talkin' to yo' crazy ass."

I snapped my head in his direction. "I'm not fuckin' crazy, aight?"

"Shittt, you could've fooled me. You get a kick outta embarrassing niggas? That's what you like to do for fun?"

I laughed to myself, then turned back around. "You're so funny, Tristan. You do look like you be eating ass, though. You look like you be getting all up in there."

"I don't eat ass." he said firmly.

I let out another laugh. This line wasn't moving and I was getting impatient. I was two seconds away from walking the fuck up out of this bitch.

"What the fuckkk," I groaned, looking at the line in front of me. There were six people ahead of me, and my stomach was touching my back. "All I want is something to eat."

"Then why the fuck you come in here, on a Friday night? You gon' be standing in this line for at least thirty minutes." he let me know.

I blew out an annoyed breath. I wasn't about to stand here for thirty damn minutes.

"Man, fuck this," I stepped out of line, then turned to leave. I didn't know where I was going next, but I knew it wasn't this soul food place. Hell nah. "What the hell am I going to eat?"

"McDonalds is always quick," Tristan said following behind me.

I smacked my lips. "Don't nobody want no nasty ass McDonalds. Fuck outta here with that shit,"

"I was just making a suggestion, shawty. No need to have an attitude."

I rolled my eyes. "Well, I left my house, drove all the way over here, just to find out I'm gonna have to wait a whole hour to get something to eat. I'm starving, so my damn bad for having an attitude with a nigga who's aimlessly following me to my damn car." I stopped walking so I could look at him.

Nigga knew he was fine as hell. I had a right mind to say fuck the food and take him back to my place. I wasn't sure if he would be up to that or not.

"Chill with me for the night. I'll cook for you." he said, easily.

For a moment, I just stood there staring at him because I didn't know what to say. I don't remember the time a nigga invited me over his house on some romantic shit. Usually, men wanted one thing, and so did I.

"Can you even cook, Tristan?" I asked, giving him a small smirk.

"I can do more than that. Come on,"

"FUCKKKKK," TRISTAN DAMN NEAR YELLED, BURYING HIS FACE IN MY neck. He was pumping in and out of me, making me dig my nails into his back.

Okay, so this nigga was he truth. He could cook, and his dick game was crazy. I don't think I'd ever got fucked *this* good.

"Just like that, baby." I moaned in his ear, causing his moans to get even louder. It was just something about him that was making me weak. Or, it could've just been him in his vulnerable state.

I loved seeing strong, masculine men broken all the way down during sex. If that shit didn't turn me on, I didn't know what did.

He lifted himself up to watch him go in and out, then we locked eyes. I felt the chills run down my spine as he looked at me. Was it too early to let this nigga know that I loved him? Man, hell nah, I was over here trippin'.

"What's my mothafuckin' name?" he asked, as my eyes rolled back.

"Daddy," I said with a small smirk on my face. Nah, he wasn't Tristan right now. He was straight giving me Daddy dick.

I could tell he was happy with my answer by the look on his face.

"What?" he asked, throwing my leg over his shoulder. "What you say my name was?"

"Mmmm, Daddy," I moaned, with my back arching into him. His dick was touching my ribcage. I knew he was rearranging everything down there.

"I'm not pulling out," he said, looking me dead in the eyes.

"Don't,"

Okay, so clearly, I wasn't thinking straight. But, that's what good dick does to you. I knew I had missed a couple of my birth control pills, but here I am, telling a nigga I just met not to pull out. Fuck was wrong with me?

"Ahh, gotttt damnnnnnnnnn!" he yelled, collapsing on top of me.

I couldn't even move. Shit was too intense. Then, there was a small knock on the door.

"Tristan?! I umm… Need you. Like now." The girl sounded frantic, and that made me raise a brow. Who the fuck is that?

"Who's that? That's not your girlfriend is it?" I asked, watching him get off of me and put his boxers back on.

"Nah, that's my cousin." he let me know, immediately putting me at ease. "What's wrong, Semaj? Why you look like that?" he asked, once the door was open.

"Your mom is here. She's downstairs, and she won't leave. I don't even know how she got in here."

"What? You serious?"

"Yes! She's creeping me out, just sitting there like a zombie. Go talk to her and get her the hell out of here,"

"Aight. Just... hide in your room until I get her ass out of here. Be ready to go when she's gone."

She let out a loud sigh. "Again? We gotta move again?"

"Yeah. We'll talk about the shit later. Just go do what I told you to do."

He shut the door, then ran a hand down his face. I could tell he was annoyed, but I wasn't going to speak on it. I mean, not right now.

"Should I leave?" I asked, sitting up in the bed.

"Nah. Not yet. Put your clothes on, though. Shit might get crazy."

He quickly threw some clothes on then walked out the door. I wasted no time putting mine back on. I had no idea what was going on, but I wasn't feeling the tone of voice he had. Shit wasn't sitting right with me.

15

TRISTAN

My mom was up to something. There was no reason that she would just pop up over here unannounced. I didn't even talk to her stupid ass, but now you wanna just come over? First off, how the fuck did she even know where we were at? She had to either be following me or Semaj and I didn't even realize it.

"What the hell you want?" I asked, standing in front of her. She looked different. She looked like she was on drugs? Or, maybe she was sick. Either way, she looked like she was losing hell weight, and her face was sunken in.

"I can't come by to talk to my son?" she asked, quietly. She wouldn't even look at me. That's how I knew everything that was about to come from her mouth was bullshit.

"I'm not ya son. Remember? We haven't talked in how long? Your son is eight. That's who you need to be worried about."

She was quiet for a moment, but then, she finally looked at me. "He can't help me right now. He's only eight, Tristan."

"I know how old the nigga is. Now get to the point before I kick yo' ass outta my house."

"I'm dying. I have lung cancer, and I don't have the money for—"

"Not my problem, Renee. You haven't talked to me in years. You treated me like shit just because my pops didn't want you. Now, that you need some money, you think you can just show up over here and I'm gonna give you some money? Nah, it doesn't work like that."

She bit the inside of her cheek. "At the end of the day, I'm still your mother, Tristan. I pushed you outta me. You *have* to help me."

I gave her the ugliest expression. "I don't have to do shit, bruh! Just like you had a son, but didn't have to be a mother, I don't have to help yo' stupid ass. Get the fuck outta my house, yo."

"This isn't your house. It's my brother's. I can stay here as long as I want," she flipped her ugly ass weave off her shoulder, then gave me a menacing look. "You're gonna give me some money, Tristan. Either we can do this the easy way, or we can do it the hard way. Your choice."

"So, you're threatening me now? You think that shit is gonna scare me or something?" I chuckled and watched her pull out a .45 from her purse.

"Like I said, it's your choice. I tried to do it the easy way, but it's sounding like you don't want that. I'd hate to have to shoot you, Tristan. I mean, I did give birth to you."

She aimed the gun at me and I wanted to punch myself for not bringing the strap downstairs with me.

"But, you didn't give birth to me," Semaj said, coming from around the corner with her gun aimed.

"Semaj, I told you to stay upstairs. What the hell you doing?"

"No. She's here to try to kill the both of us. That sob story she just gave you was probably bullshit. She was gonna shoot you regardless."

Renee smiled at her. "Maybe I should kill your uppity ass first. I never liked you, anyway."

"The feeling is definitely mutual, Renee. I should've known you were following me when I saw you at the mall the other day. You thought I didn't see you, but I did."

The fuck? So, Semaj saw Renee but didn't think it would've been a good idea to tell me? What kinda shit?

"So fuckin' what? I'm not the only person that's watching your every move. It doesn't matter what you do, or where you go. They're gonna find you, then finally put a bullet through your precious little head like they tried to do at the funeral. Hopefully, this time, they won't miss." Renee gave Semaj a wicked smile, and before I knew it, Semaj pulled the trigger, hitting Renee right in the throat.

"Stupid ass bitch," Semaj spat.

A nigga was at a loss for words right now. I didn't expect none of this shit to happen. I mean, not today. Then, Semaj didn't even seem bothered with what she'd just done. Shit was throwing me off a little.

"Shit," I muttered, looking at what used to be my mom. The only reason I felt a little remorse was because her youngest was gonna have to grow up without a mom. Honestly, I was probably doing him a favor, anyway. "We gotta go. We gotta get the fuck outta here."

"For what? She said—"

"I don't give a fuck what she said, Semaj! We need to go! Get ya shit."

"Again? We gotta do this again? I'm tired of running! I'm tired of doing all of this shit!"

I ignored her as I walked back up the stairs to get Alaya. I was gonna have to drop her ass off ASAP. I didn't know if what Renee was talking about was true, but I wasn't gonna sit around waiting for mothafuckas to try to kill us.

"You okay?" Alaya asked, looking like she was scared out of her mind.

"Nah, not really. Get all ya shit, though. We leaving."

"Where we going?"

I gave her a blank stare. She was asking too many damn questions for me.

"Just get the fuck up. We don't got all day."

She rolled her eyes, then got off the bed. She slid her shoes on and followed right behind me. She was still asking questions the whole time we walked down the stairs, but I was ignoring her ass. There was too much shit to worry about right now.

Semaj was standing by the couch, looking at my mom's dead body when I made it back downstairs.

"Semaj," I said, causing her to look up at me. "What the hell are you doing?"

"Am I going to go to jail? What's gonna happen when they find her dead body just laying here? Are they gonna know I'm the one who killed her?"

"Who is that?" Alaya asked, with fear all in her voice. "Who is that, Tristan?!"

"Man, chill. That wasn't nobody important. I'll call somebody to come clean everything up. They won't even know she's dead."

Semaj still just stood there not moving. I was starting to get annoyed. I knew she was feeling some type of way because she just killed somebody, but damn. She knew we had shit to do. We needed to get the fuck outta here.

"Y'all aren't gonna kill me too, are y'all? Lemme know now before I go anywhere with—"

"Man, shut up, Alaya. I just need you to be quiet right now. Semaj, let's go. You still standing there like we don't have shit to do."

She finally looked up at me, then slowly walked towards the door. "I'm ready."

As she opened the door, I made sure I had everything I needed.

POP! POP! POP!

Semaj fell to the floor and me and Alaya ducked for cover.

"Shit!" I yelled, hearing the gunshots coming from all over. "Semaj?! Semaj, get the hell up!" I could see her bleeding, but I had no idea where the blood was coming from. I was hoping and praying that she wasn't hurt too bad.

"What the hell, Tristan?! I didn't sign up for this!" Alaya yelled.

"Chill shawty, go to the garage!"

"What? I don't know where the damn garage is!"

"Go to the kitchen! Just get ya ass in the kitchen!" I didn't wait to see what the hell she was about to do. Gunshots were flying, Semaj was laid out on the floor, and I needed to do something quick.

I quickly pulled my strap out and made my way to the door. I saw a nigga standing right by the bushes. I put two bullets in his head and ended his life. After that, I quickly shut the door, and picked Semaj up off the floor. From the looks of it, the bullet had just grazed her arm, but she was over here acting like she was dead.

"Come on, Semaj. You aight. We need to get the fuck outta here."

She opened her eyes to look at me. "No. Just leave me here to die. You'll be better off without me."

I smacked my lips. "You better come the fuck on before I leave yo' stupid ass. You trippin'."

"It hurts!"

"Girl, it's gonna hurt! You just got shot! Now come on!" I didn't wait for her to respond as I made my way to the garage. Alaya was already standing at the door waiting for us.

"What you got going on, Tristan? I wouldn't have come over here if I would've known I was gonna get shot at. What the hell is this?!" she asked.

I tuned her ass out. I understood where she was coming from, but the only thing I could think of right now was getting the fuck away from here right now. I didn't know who all my mom had lead over here, but I wasn't about to find out.

"I'm going to dieee," Semaj groaned, coming around the corner, holding her arm. "Tell Trinity I love her."

I let out a loud sigh. "Aight, so both of y'all go get in the car right now. We don't have time to be standing around talking and shit!"

I swung the garage door open, and we all got in the car. Semaj got in the front and Alaya got in the back. Semaj was still complaining how she was dying, Alaya was talking shit about how she didn't plan on dying tonight, and I swear to God, I was about to lose my mind. How the hell was I gonna get the fuck out of this garage without getting shot?

"Aye y'all," I said, getting both of their attention. "Keep your heads down."

"Huh? Why? Are we gonna get shot?" Alaya asked.

"It's a possibility."

"Oh God," Semaj groaned. "I don't need to get shot again. I don't even know if I'm gonna survive this. I'm already losing too much blood! Get me to the hospital, Tristan!"

I ignored her and pushed the button to let the garage up. As soon as the door was all the way up, the shooting started back up again. I stepped on the gas and backed out the garage. The bullets were hitting the car, but I was doing everything in my power not to let any of us get hit.

"Yo, what the fuck?!" Alaya yelled. "I didn't sign up for this dumb ass shit!"

There was a nigga standing in the yard, so I put the car back in drive and ran over that nigga. I didn't know if I killed his ass or not, but I was hoping I did.

"Fuck ass nigga," I muttered, heading in the direction of the hospital.

"Wow, this is some crazy ass shit. What the hell am I gonna do about my car? What if they shoot my shit up?! Then what, Tristan? Are you gonna replace it? Huh?!" Alaya yelled as I looked at her in the rearview mirror.

"Man, chill. Your car ain't what's important right now."

"Exactly! I'm over here about to die and you're worried about your damn car?!" Semaj snapped.

"Girl, fuck you. I don't even know yo' ass! My car is important! I paid for that shit with my own money. Why the fuck wouldn't my shit be important? Man, y'all got me so fucked up right now!"

"Shut up with all that. If your car is messed up, I'll pay to get it fixed, aight? It really ain't that serious right now." I had a right mind to drop her ass off somewhere, but I needed to get Semaj's dramatic ass to the hospital first.

"You better, nigga. This shit is so crazy. All I wanted was dick. I would've took my ass home if I knew all this shit was gonna happen. Swear to God if I die tonight because of y'all, I'm coming back from the dead to haunt you. I'm gonna haunt you until the day you die, nigga."

I let out a small chuckle, but I didn't say shit to her. She was talking too damn much. Shit was getting annoying as fuck. As soon as I got Semaj to the hospital, I was dropping Alaya the fuck off. I wasn't gonna be able to deal with her too much longer.

16

TRINITY

"How the fuck did I accidentally get into a relationship?" I muttered to myself, as I looked down at my phone. Yeah, I was feeling Two, but I damn sure wasn't looking for a relationship. I don't even remember him saying anything about being together. He just started telling people I was his girlfriend and shit.

Right now, we were supposed to be watching movies, but his ass fell asleep during the first one. I wanted to get something to eat, but his ass was snoring loud as fuck. I knew he wasn't waking up anytime soon.

That's when my phone started ringing, with Tristan's name popping up on the screen. What the hell was this nigga even calling me for? I had a right mind to ignore him, but maybe it was important.

"Hello?" I said quietly, so I wouldn't wake up Two's crazy ass.

"Aye, umm... Semaj got shot. I just dropped her off at the hospital."

My brows came together and the front door swung open, and in walked Trap like he lived here and shit.

"What? When the hell did this happen? Is she okay? Was it bad?" As I was asking question after question, I was trying to get up from under Two. This nigga was heavy as hell.

"What's up, Trinity?" Trap asked once I finally got Two's heavy ass legs off of me.

"Hey," I said, looking around for my shoes. I didn't have time to just be standing here. I needed to be at the hospital. I wish Tristan would've called me as soon as it happened.

"Yeah, I think she's gonna be good. It only hit her in the arm, but you know she's dramatic as fuck. I got some shit to handle so I had to leave."

I nodded like he could see me. I saw my shoes, slipped them on, and looked around for my keys. That's when I remembered that Two came and picked me up.

"Okay. I'm about to head over there right now."

"Aight, bet." he ended the call and I nudged Two, trying to wake him up. This nigga was knocked out like he'd been working his entire life.

"Nigga, wake the hell up. I need to get to the hospital!"

"Man, go on somewhere. I'm tired." he said without even opening his eyes.

"I don't give a fuck about you being tired, nigga! My friend is in the hospital!"

He ignored me, then eventually he started snoring again. I blew out an annoyed breath and thought about ways to get to the hospital. I could've called an Uber, but I really didn't wanna pay for it. I could get there for free if Two woke his stupid ass up.

Trap came back into the living room, looking down at his phone, and that's when I decided to just ask him to take me. I didn't want to, but that was the only way I was gonna get there without paying for it.

"Hey, could you give me a ride to the hospital, please?" I asked, watching him look at me.

"The hospital?"

"Yeah… Semaj got shot."

He lifted a brow. "My Semaj?"

Your Semaj? Nigga, when the fuck that happen?

"Umm… I only know one Semaj, so…"

"Yeah, come on." He was out the door before I could even say anything back to him. I could see the concern written all over his face. I thought it was kinda cute, but I made a mental note to ask Semaj what was going on between them when I made it to the hospital.

"You know how to get there, right?" I asked, sliding in the passenger seat of his car.

"Yeah," he chuckled. "What happened, though? She good?"

I shrugged. "I have no idea. Her cousin called me to tell me where she was at, but the only information he gave me was that she got shot in the arm."

"That's it? Nowhere else?"

"I think. I'm not completely sure."

He nodded, then sped down the street. Honestly, this was the most awkward car ride I think I'd ever had. He wasn't talking to me, I wasn't talking to him, and he didn't have the music playing. It was silent in the car. I had a right mind to turn the radio on, but I didn't want him to get mad at me.

"So, do you always ride in silence like this?" I asked, causing him to glance at me.

"Sometimes. The radio plays the same four songs over and over and that shit annoying. Plus, I think better when the car is silent. That ain't a problem for you, is it?"

"I mean, it's a little awkward. I'm not used to riding in silence like this." He just shrugged. He didn't even bother saying anything back to me. "So, what's going on with you and Semaj? Are y'all like together or something?"

He chuckled and glanced at me, then quickly averted his attention back to the road. "You always this talkative? I mean, I don't really be around you and Two like that, but when I do, it doesn't seem like you be talking this much."

"I talk more when I'm around him. But, you know, I was just trying to make conversation with you. Shit, play some music. I won't talk anymore. And don't think I didn't notice you trying to dodge the question I just asked you about Semaj."

"Do I ask you about you and my brother?"

I opened my mouth to say something, but nothing came out. He didn't ask about me and his brother, but that wasn't the point. Semaj was my best friend, so of course I was gonna ask about it. Especially since she didn't even like hood niggas like him.

"We're two different people, *Mega*."

He snapped his head in my direction and twisted his mouth. "Man, don't call me that shit. It doesn't even sound right coming outta your mouth."

"So, Semaj can call you that, but I can't?"

"Hell yeah. I'm not fucking you." he said easily as my mouth fell open.

So, they were fucking? And Semaj didn't even tell me? When the hell did this happen?

"What?!" I said excitedly. "Y'all are having sex?"

"Man," he groaned. "Chill. What you so excited for? Don't sit there and act like you didn't know the shit was gonna happen."

"Nigga, I didn't know it was gonna happen! You know how Semaj is. She doesn't even like—"

"Yo, if I turn the radio on, will you shut the hell up? You talking way too much right now."

I gave him the ugliest expression. Who the hell did this nigga think he was?

"Okay, when I asked you to turn the radio on, you had a problem with it. Now that I wanna talk, that's a problem, too? I swear, niggas are never satisfied." I said, folding my arms.

"Man, you didn't ask me to turn on shit. You asked if I listen to the radio. Gahh damn, I didn't know you talked this damn much. That shit crazy."

"What? So now, all of a sudden, I talk too much? I'm allowed to talk, though. You're the one—"

He turned the radio up as loud as it would go and I just sat there looking at him like he was crazy. He was so damn rude. I know he didn't act like this when he was around Semaj because she would probably cuss his rude ass out.

I didn't say anything to him the rest of the ride to the hospital. Honestly, I was just ready to get out of the car and get away from him.

I wish Two would've woke his ass up. Then I wouldn't have to go through no shit like this.

When we finally made it to the hospital, I damn near ran inside. I didn't bother waiting on Trap's ass because right now, he wasn't one of my favorite people. I was beyond excited when they told me Semaj was okay and could have visitors.

She was just lying in the bed watching TV when I walked in. Once she saw me, she gave me the biggest smile.

"Hey," she said quietly. "I almost died today."

I rolled my eyes. "Girl hush. You're so dramatic. You barely got hit."

"So! That shit was scary as hell! Tristan's mom came trying to kill us! I had to shoot her!"

"Shhh!" I snapped, looking around. "You can't just say stuff like that here."

"You could've waited for me, bruh." Trap said, walking in the room. I fought the urge to roll my eyes again.

"Okay? And you could've been nicer to me on the car ride over here, but you weren't, were you?"

He smacked his lips. "Man, you were talking too damn much."

I waved him off, then turned my attention to Semaj. "So, when the hell were you gonna tell me that y'all are fucking?" I folded my arms and watched as Semaj's eyes got big.

"You told her?!" she shrieked.

He shrugged and stuffed his hands in his pockets. "It slipped. It was an accident."

"So, you weren't gonna tell me? Wow, Semaj. I'm hurt right now." I brought my hand to my chest, pretending like my feelings were actually hurt, and she ran a hand through her hair.

"Okay, so, I almost died. We should not be talking about who I'm having sex with. We should be talking about people from my family trying to kill me."

Trap went to sit in the chair next to her bed, then took her hand in his.

"What happened, baby?"

Honestly, I didn't know what to say or think. This nigga really just came out of nowhere and snatched her heart right outta her chest. I was even over here blushing at the gesture he just did. It was always some cute ass shit when a hood nigga started to catch feelings.

"Okay so first," Semaj started, making me give her my full attention. "I was just sitting on the couch, trying to find something to watch. Then, there was knocking at the door. I didn't expect it to be my cousin's mom. Long story short, she forced her way into the house, talked to my cousin a little bit, then pulled her gun out! On her own son!"

Once again, my mouth fell open. I knew the story about Tristan and Renee. I never thought she would go as far as trying to kill him though. At the end of the day, that's still your child. You pushed this baby out of you.

"Really? She was really gonna shoot Tristan?" I asked and she nodded.

"Yep. She was saying how she needed money, and how Tristan basically had to give it to her because she was his mom and stuff. I was still downstairs because I felt like she was gonna do some sneaky stuff. It was a good thing I was in the kitchen, though. After she pulled out her gun, I pulled mine out and aimed it at her." she said.

"Oh shit," I laughed. "Who the hell you think you are?"

Semaj let out a loud chuckle. "Shut up. But anyway, she started telling me that there are people watching my every move and I got tired of hearing her talk, so I shot her. Hit her ass right in the neck."

I felt like I didn't know my best friend anymore. Ever since her dad died, and Trap came into her life? She's been acting like a totally different person.

"You didn't throw up this time?" Trap asked her.

She shook her head. "Nope. You were so right. The more you shoot, the better it gets. I'm ready for the rest of the family to try to come at me so I can shoot them, too. Since they don't know how to leave me alone."

"Let's hope you won't have to do that, though," I said, hoping Trap would agree with me, but he didn't.

"Nah, that shit gonna happen again. They not gonna stop no time soon."

I wanted to hit him in the back of his head to tell him to shut the hell up, but I didn't. I would feel some type of way if a bitch did that to my nigga, so I wouldn't dare do that.

"Thanks, because that makes me feel so much better," she spat, sarcastically.

"I mean, I was just saying. There ain't no reason to lie to you, shawty."

Just as Semaj opened her mouth to say something, my phone started ringing in my hand. I rolled my eyes when I saw it was only Two calling. So, now his nigga wanted to be up, and worrying about what the hell I was doing?

"Hello?" I sighed into the phone.

"Aye, where the hell you at? You just gon' leave like we weren't watching—"

"Nigga, my friend got shot. I tried to wake you up, but you told me to leave you alone."

He let out a loud yawn. "Shit. I don't even remember that. My bad, ma. I would've took you to see her and shit. A nigga been tired as hell, lately."

"Mhm," I said, not really giving a damn. He hasn't been doing shit, so why the hell is he so tired?

"Semaj got shot?"

"Yes, nigga. She's good though. Your brother is up here making sure she's good."

He let out a small laugh. "Of course, he is. Pussy whipped ass nigga."

"What? You're pussy whipped, too. Don't try to act like—"

"Man, no the fuck I'm not. Don't lie on me."

"But, you tell me you're falling in love with the pussy all the time though. So, you be lying to me? You're a liar, Two?"

"Nah. But sometimes, I just be talking. You shouldn't take everything I say serious, Trinity."

I chuckled to myself. "Exactly. You're a lying ass nigga just like the rest of them. Anyways, I'll call you later. I should be focused on my friend right now."

I ended the call before he could respond. I just didn't feel like talking to him right now. When I called him back later, I was going to tell him that I didn't wanna be in a relationship with his ass, either.

I glanced over at Trap and Semaj who were engaging in their own conversation. The way he looked at her warmed my heart. She deserved a nigga that was all for her, even though it was a little weird to see her with a hood nigga.

"What's up?" Tristan asked as he walked into the room.

I smiled at him. He was so cute. If I wouldn't have been with Antonio, I would've definitely given him a chance.

"Hey, Tristan. You look nice."

He smiled at me as Trap turned around and stood up. Once Tritan saw Trap standing, his entire demeanor changed, and before I knew it, they both had their guns drawn and aimed at each other.

"The fuck you got this bitch ass nigga in here for, Semaj? You know him?" Tristan asked, with his finger hovering over the trigger.

Semaj was too shocked for words just like I was.

"Fuck you all up in her business for, nigga? You think I'd be here for no reason? The better question is, why *you're* here, pussy."

Semaj quickly got out of the bed and stood between them.

"Stop it!" she yelled, trying to lower Trap's gun. He looked at her like she was crazy.

"You fuckin' this nigga too?"

She shook her head. "No! He's my cousin!" He ignored her and still had his gun aimed at Tristan. The crazy part was, neither of them had an ounce of fear in their eyes. Not me, though. I was over here about to shit bricks. "Mega?!" Semaj shrieked, causing him to finally look at her.

They stared each other down for a couple seconds, then he finally lowered his gun. "Pussy ass east side nigga," he spat. "I'll hit you up later, Semmy," He walked past Tristan and out the room completely.

"That's ya boyfriend?" Tristan asked, putting his gun back in the waist of his pants. He gave her a cold look and she shook her head.

"No, he's not."

"Why the fuck was he in here? How you know him?"

My brows came together. Tristan looked like he was ready to fight Semaj. I didn't know if he was the type of nigga to put his hands on women, but I was prepared to fight that nigga like he stole something from me if he did.

"He's a friend, Tristan. I'm not allowed to have those either? Or no, are you gonna tell me he's out here trying to kill me too? He wants some of my money?" Semaj rolled her eyes.

"Nah. I don't fuck with that nigga. You shouldn't either."

"Why though? What did he do to you?" I asked, wondering if he felt the same way about Two.

"That shit ain't important."

"Just like how the people I hang out with isn't important to you. You're not going to tell me who I can and can't hang with." she said, with the attitude dripping from her voice.

I could tell by the look that was on his face that he didn't wanna go back and forth with her.

He shrugged. "Aight, Semaj. You got it. Don't come crying to me when—"

"I'm not going to come crying to you!"

He looked at her for a moment before he turned to leave. "I'll be in the car. Check yourself out." He was out the door before we could even say anything back to him.

"Now, I wanna know what happened between them. I didn't even know they knew each other." I said, watching her swing her legs off the bed.

"I'm really high." she giggled.

I lifted a brow. "Girl, hush. You don't even know what being high feels like."

"Yes I do, because Mega showed me." She smiled as she made her way over to me.

"You smoked with him?" I damn near yelled. "You are so fake. You would never smoke with me when I would—"

"I didn't smoke anything," she let me know. "It was in the brownie he made."

"So, you ate an edible."

"That's what they're called? I was just going to call it a weed brownie or something. Such a cute name for it."

I fought the urge to laugh as I followed behind her out the room. I didn't know if she checked herself or not, but she was walking towards the entrance of the hospital like she did. I was t about to say anything about it.

"Bitch, I wanna know how the dick was. I can't believe you tried to hide it from me!"

She looked at me through wide eyes. "I wasn't trying to hide it from you. What, you wanted me to call you right after it happened?"

"Bitch yes!"

She twisted her face up. "I'm not going to call you every time o have sex, Trinity. Just like how I don't want you to call me and tell me about your sex life. But, I will say this," she said, flipping her hair from her shoulder. "It was way better than Marcus. Way better."

"Girl," I laughed. "I could've told you it was gonna be better. Hood niggas always got the best dick. But, they come with hella problems."

"All men come with problems. I don't wanna deal with any of them."

"So, are you and Mega gonna be a couple? Your first *grown* boyfriend?"

She shook her head. "Oh God, no. I would never. He's not my type. I think I'll just keep him around for sex, though. That's the best thing about him."

I thought about telling her how Trap wasn't going to go for that, but I'd let her find that out on her own. He was already acting sprung over her, and they'd only had sex once. Semaj is about to be in for a rude awakening.

TWO

ONE MONTH LATER

"Let's go out to eat tonight," Destiny said, sitting up in the bed.

"Why can't we just order something?" I asked, not wanting to go anywhere where people could see me with her.

"You're so lazy," she said, rolling her eyes. "You always just wanna order something. You act like you don't wanna take me on dates and shit. You got a girlfriend you tryna hide from me?"

I waved her off. "Hell no."

But actually, that's exactly what it was. I didn't even know I wanted to get with Trinity, but the shit just happened. She was better than any of the bitches I fucked with, and she had a good head on her shoulders. She knew what she wanted out of life. All the other bitches just like fucking with me because they want the money. That's why I wasn't taking bitches serious in the first place.

"Then why don't you ever wanna go out with me? You don't even have to pay."

"Because I'm not in the mood, shawty. It doesn't have anything to do with you."

"Whatever, Two. You're probably hiding from a girl. But whatever, I'll just order some food. Are you gonna go pick it up, or you're not in the mood to do that either?"

I sighed to myself. "Man, if you want me to go pick it up, I will. You over there trippin'."

"What? If I want you to? I want you to take me out, but you can't do that?"

I ran a hand down my face. "What's the problem, Destiny? What you really mad at?"

"Why do you act like you don't wanna be with me? Am I not good enough or something?"

"Man, What? I been told you I didn't want a relationship—"

"Why? So you can fuck other bitches? Huh?"

"I don't understand what you're mad at. I'm fucking you, right? Man, you were fucking other niggas too. You got pregnant with another nigga's baby. But, now it's a problem?"

"I just don't feel like we're making any progress. Like, is all we're gonna do is fuck?"

Why the hell did this bitch want a relationship so bad? Why couldn't she just be happy with what we were doing? What was the problem?

"I mean, that's what I planned on. You really can't feel no type of way because I already told you what it was from jump."

"Wow," she scoffed, shaking her head. "All That money I gave you, and I'm still not good enough to be the only woman in your life. I don't even know why I try with niggas." She shook her head and I looked at her ass like she was crazy.

Did she really think her giving me some money was gonna make me wanna be with her? The hell kinda nigga did she think I was?

"So, you gave me the money because you thought it was gonna make me wanna be with you?"

"I mean, no, but I thought it would at least help. This shit is so crazy." She started picking at her nails, and my phone vibrated beside me.

I glanced at it and saw it was Trinity calling, so I quickly tried to put it on silent, but Destiny was watching me.

"Who's that calling you, Two? Your other bitches?"

"Man, I don't have any other bitches. Stop saying that dumb shit."

"Then answer the phone. If you don't have any other bitches, then answer your phone right now."

I smacked my lips and quickly got out of the bed. Why the hell was I sitting here going back and forth with her like she was my bitch? I didn't have to explain shit to her. Fuck she thought this was?

"I'm out. I'll hit you up later," I said, putting my shoes on and making my way towards the door.

"Really? Are you serious? See, that's how I know it's another bitch calling you! Look at how you're acting!" She ran behind me, and I let out an annoyed breath.

"You're not my bitch, Destiny! I don't have to explain shit to you! I don't have to argue with you either! What the fuck are you mad for? I spend time with you, right? I fuck you, right? I listen to all your dumb ass stories about how work went, right? Why you gotta go and start some shit? I was having a good day until you started running your mouth bruh."

"Whatever, Two. You're a liar. I don't even know why I played myself, thinking you would stop being childish and actually get into a relationship with me. This is no one's fault but my own."

"Childish? Man, get the fuck outta here with that shit. What's childish is you thinking a little bit of money was gonna make me wanna be with you. You crazy as fuck, shawty. But I'll hit you up later."

I didn't plan on hitting her ass up any more after today. She was trippin'.

"I want my money back, then." she said, folding her arms.

"Nah, bruh. That shit mine now." I made my way to the car with her following and yelling behind me.

"Give me my money back or I'm gonna call the police!" I ignored her and kept walking. I didn't know why the fuck she thought calling the police was really gonna scare me. Call them, bitch. I don't give a fuck.

As soon as I pulled out of her driveway, I called Trinity back.

"I'm so glad you called me back," she said. "I thought you were somewhere sleeping."

"Nah, I was outside and left my phone in the house." I quickly lied.

"Where you at? You never leave your phone anywhere."

"I was at my home boy's crib. I'm heading home now, though."

"Great. I'll meet you there," She ended the call and I let out a sigh of relief. I don't know what the hell she would do if she found out I was cheating, but I honestly didn't wanna find out.

I didn't plan on cheating on Trinity. I didn't know Destiny was gonna constantly want dick either. The only reason I was still dealing with Destiny was because I thought she was gonna give me some more money and shit. Clearly, shit wasn't about to go down like that.

I planned on that being the last time I fucked with Destiny, though. Shawty seemed a little off, and plus, I needed to be a better nigga to Trinity.

My phone began vibrating, and it was no one but Destiny calling me. I declined the call, then blocked her number. I didn't need her ass calling me while I was with Trinity. That shit was a disaster waiting to happen.

"Not about to get me caught up, bitch," I muttered to myself as my phone rang again. I thought it was Destiny calling but it was just my brother. "What's good, nigga? Where you at?"

"Bruh," he said, sounding like he was out of breath. "Man, tell me why me and Spazz went to the gas station and shit and all the east side niggas over here."

"Word? Which gas station y'all at?"

"Shit, the one on the west. Shell, bruh."

"Nigga, what the hell you doing? I know y'all not out there running."

He laughed. "Nah, I jogged into the store to pay for my gas and I'm tired as hell. I'm outta shape like shit. I need to get my ass in a gym or some shit."

I busted a U-turn in the middle of the road and headed to where Trap was.

"You do need to get in the gym if you sound like that from jogging. Get ya shit together. It's probably all that nasty ass McDonalds you always eating."

"Nigga. you eat McDonalds just as much as I do. The fuck that gotta do with anything."

"Man, fuck all that. I'm going vegan. All this fast food and shit is bad for us."

"Whattt?" he laughed. "Nigga, get the fuck outta here with that shit. Everything is bad for you. But, good luck with that going vegan shit. I would never try it."

Luckily, I wasn't too far from where Trap was. When I pulled up, it looked like the east side niggas were having a big ass meeting and just chillin' at the damn gas station. I slowly rode past all of them, making sure they all saw me mugging them, then parked next to Trap and Spazz. They both got out the car when they saw me.

"Whose car is this?" I asked, looking at the all-white BMW they were riding in.

"Shit, I don't know," Spazz said. "I stole this shit earlier."

"For real? From where? You just going around stealing cars and shit now?"

"Hell yeah," he nodded. "I'm gonna sell this shit."

"I just wanted to test drive the shit, but his ass been acting stingy with the shit since he got it," Trap chimed in.

"Nigga, you can't drive! You gon' fuck the car up before I even get to sell it!"

"Fuck you. I'm a great driver. My shit be smooth as hell."

"East side nigga!" I heard a nigga yell from across the parking lot. Those niggas wanted problems. What the hell they doing posted up on the west side?

"They came over here to start some shit," Spazz said. "Why else would they all be on the west side?"

"Exactly what I was thinking," I said, watching a black truck pull up beside us. The same nigga from the gym that day hopped out, looking like he was ready for some action.

"What's up, nigga?" I heard him say. "You was talkin' that hot shit when we were at the gym. You lookin' real scared and shit, now."

I chuckled to myself. Niggas were crazy.

I didn't say anything as I pulled out the strap. I shot him twice in the chest, and once in the head. The driver of the car he had hopped out of sped off, then me, Trap, and Spazz all got in my car and sped off too.

"See, there you go with that shit," Spazz said. "I knew something was gonna go down. I knew it as soon as Trap called your crazy ass."

I shrugged. "Them niggas wanted that shit to happen. Why the fuck else would they just be posted like that? I was supposed to let that nigga talk to me crazy? Nah, bruh."

I glanced over at Trap who wasn't saying anything. That nigga was too busy in his phone, probably texting Semaj.

"Yo," he said, finally looking up from his phone. "This shit is crazy, though. You the only mothafucka that I know that will kill someone in broad daylight. You didn't even flinch after it happened."

"That nigga wanted to die. That's not my problem." I shrugged.

"Nah," Spazz laughed. "You're just crazy. You killed him and his brother."

"Like I said, that's not my problem."

We drove for about three hours until we reached the small house we had in Ashville. I dropped the car off, dropped the guns I had on me off, then we got in a completely different car. After that, we left again, and headed back to Atlanta.

"All this shit could've been avoided," Trap said with a loud yawn.

"Nigga, shut up. You acting like this the first time I've ever did this shit. It ain't even that serious,"

"Since when has killing someone ever not been serious? Yo, I swear something is wrong with you. You were probably dropped on your head as a baby and shit." Spazz said, making Trap laugh.

"Shit, he probably was. Nigga be doing some dumb ass shit."

I ignored them as I drove. The only thing I was thinking about was Trinity. She was probably mad as hell that I hadn't shown up yet. I pulled my phone out of my pocket to send her a quick text, but I'd already had one from her, followed by hella missed calls.

Trin: I don't know what the fuck you got going on, but I'm not here for it. Stay with whatever hoe that's got your attention.

"Damn, man." I muttered. I wasn't even with a bitch, but I already knew it was going to be hard trying to explain that shit to Trinity.

18

SEMAJ

"I'm dying, Trinity," I groaned, feeling her sit next to me on the bed.

"Girl," she laughed. "Get the hell up. Ain't nothing wrong with you. You just don't wanna go out with me tonight,"

I mean, that was partly true. I really didn't want to go out with her. I didn't want to put on the outfit she had laid out for me, I didn't want to put on the heels that were way too high, and I didn't want to be around too many people.

"I've been throwing up all day. I can't eat anything, and now I'm starving. I think I have a stomach bug."

She snatched the covers from off my head so she could look at me.

"Throwing up?" she asked, with an arched eyebrow.

"Yes. That's what I just said."

"When's the last time you had your period?"

This time, I sat up to look at her. "I don't know. Last month was the last time I remember being on my period. What does that have to do with—"

"Get up. Put some clothes on."

"Why? Why won't you just let me lay here in bed? I told you I don't feel good and—"

"Bitch, you don't feel good because you're pregnant. Now, come on. We're going to get some tests."

"Pregnant?" I chuckled. "No. I'm definitely not pregnant."

She crossed her arms as she looked at me. "Does your boyfriend use condoms?"

"Mega isn't my boyfriend. And no. He doesn't but—"

"Exactly. Get your ass up and come on."

I sighed loudly, but the covers off me and got out of bed.

"This isn't fair. Why can't you go get it yourself?" I pouted, looking around the room for something to put on.

"Because I'm not the one that's pregnant, Semaj. Just come on, girl."

It took us fifteen minutes to get to the store, and I was dreading getting out. The entire car ride, I thought I was going to throw up all over Trinity's car. Also, Trinity's phone rang every two minutes, but she kept ignoring it.

"Are you and Maurice having problems?" I asked, stepping out of the car.

"Fuck him. I just feel like he has other bitches. Yesterday, I called him, he didn't answer, but he called me right back. I told him I was going to his house, and this nigga never showed up! I was calling him, and he wasn't answering, but now he wants to talk? Nah nigga, where the fuck were you yesterday? With some bitch."

I laughed to myself. "Just because he wasn't answering, that doesn't mean he was with another woman."

"I can feel it, Semaj. It feels like he's hiding something from me. But, that's not the part that's pissing me off. What's pissing me off is I didn't even wanna be in a relationship. Shit, I just got outta one. I wouldn't even care if he had other bitches if we weren't together. Niggas are so stupid, bruh."

"Well, maybe you should ask him about it." I suggested.

"Hell no. So he can lie to me? I don't got time for it. All men are liars."

"Mega isn't a liar," I smiled.

"Yes, he is. You just haven't caught him yet."

I twisted my mouth, but decided to keep my thoughts to myself. I truly didn't think Mega was lying to me. He didn't have anything to lie about.

"I've never bought one of these," I said quietly as Trinity picked up three different pregnancy test. "I don't even know how they work."

"Girl," she laughed. "All you do is pee on the shit and it'll tell you if you're pregnant or not. It's pretty simple, actually."

Once she turned her back to me, I rolled my eyes. This was the dumbest thing ever. Why didn't she just believe that I had a stomach bug? Why did she have to be extra and buy pregnancy tests?

"I'm not even pregnant." I muttered.

"Hush. Once you find out if you're pregnant or not, I promise you'll feel a lot better."

"How? This pregnancy test is going to make the puking stop? Or what about the nausea?" I crossed my arms and waited for her to respond.

"No. I'm talking mentally, bitch." She sat the tests on the counter so we could pay for them.

"Hey Trinity," the cashier smiled. "I haven't seen you in so long."

"Hey Destiny," Trinity went around the counter to hug her like they were the best of friends. "Semaj this is my cousin Destiny, Destiny this is my best friend Semaj."

I gave her a small smile and waved and she just rolled her eyes. Whatever. I didn't like being friends with other women, anyway.

"How are you and Maurice?" she asked Trinity, causing me to raise a brow. I wondered how she even knew about him, because the way they just hugged, they hadn't seen each other in a long time. So, that made me feel like they weren't talking either.

"We're good," Trinity lied with a smile. "We're always good."

"Mhm. That's so good to hear." I could hear the displeasure in her voice, but I didn't think Trinity caught it like I did.

We paid for the tests, then we were out of there as quickly as we came.

"I've never heard you talk about Destiny," I said when we got back to the car.

"I don't fuck with her. That's why."

"Y'all looked like the best of friends to me. How does she know about you and Maurice? You told her?"

She shook her head. "No. I haven't told her shit about that nigga. I don't even talk to her."

"So, you don't think it's weird that she knew about him? Called him by his real name and everything."

Trinity was quiet for a moment, probably because she was now thinking the same thing she was thinking.

"You're right. Then, did you see the way she looked at me when I told her we're good? She knows him. She has to." she said, with a light nod.

"You sure about that? I mean, maybe she—

"No, Semaj. She knows him. I don't know how, but there's no way she would bring him up. She shouldn't even know that I'm messing with him. The last boyfriend I told her about was Antonio."

"Do you post him on social media?" I questioned, getting hit with a wave of nausea.

"Hell no. I'm not posting a nigga on social media until I have a ring. Fuck that."

That was understandable. I didn't want to post my man at all... you know, whenever I got one.

"I'm gonna puke," I groaned, as she looked over at me.

"Please don't throw up in my car, Semaj." she begged, speeding up a little.

"You driving crazy is making me feel worse,"

"Bitch I'm going forty-five. Find a bag or something if you feel like throwing up."

"Trinity, you don't have any bags in here!"

Trinity made sure to keep her car as clean as possible. She didn't even have small trash bags laying around.

"Well shit, put your head out the window!"

I groaned and closed my eyes. I hated feeling like this, and I couldn't wait until whatever this was, passed.

About five minutes later, we got back to my place and Trinity forced me in the bathroom.

"I don't even know what to do," I said looking at the test I was holding in my hand.

"Pee on it, Semaj. Why are you turning this into something it doesn't have to be?"

"So, I just pee? That's it?"

She nodded. "Yes."

"We'll get out so I can do it."

She stepped out the bathroom and closed the door behind her. I was dreading taking this test. I was starting to wish she didn't even come over because I could've still been lying in bed right now.

I finally took a deep breath and pulled my pants down so I could pee. A little got on my hand, but I expected that to happen. Once I was finished, I sat it on the counter, flushed the toilet, and washed my hands. Trinity cane through the door with a smile on her face.

"So, what did it say?" she asked as I dried my hands.

"I don't know. I haven't looked. But, don't I have to wait like five minutes or something? Where are the directions? Why didn't we read them?"

"It's probably three minutes. Lemme see it." I handed it to her, then left the bathroom. I was starving, but couldn't eat anything because nothing would stay down.

I sighed to myself as Trinity came out the bathroom with a big smile on her face.

"Congrats, bitch. I'm gonna be an auntie," She tossed me the pregnancy test, and I saw the plus sign on it.

"No," I said shaking my head. "This can't be right."

"Well it is. I told you."

I could feel my heart drumming in my ears. Pregnant? By Mega? And we're not even in a relationship? I've only known this man for a couple of months. I didn't know how to feel right now.

"Maybe this test was broke," I said, trying to convince myself that I wasn't pregnant.

"It wasn't broke. Stop being in denial. You're pregnant, boo. You're about to have a little Mega running around here."

I twisted my face up because I didn't like the way it sounded. I was nowhere near ready for a baby. Shit, who's to say Mega was ready for a baby either? It wouldn't surprise me if he told me to get rid of it.

"Shit," I muttered to myself. "I have to tell Mega."

"Yeah girl, handle that. I'm gonna go home and find something else to do since my best friend is pregnant and won't go out with me."

I fought the urge to roll my eyes as she left.

Pregnant.

I couldn't believe I'd let this happen. I should've been on birth control or something. I really wasn't thinking.

I sighed to myself and pulled out my phone to call Mega. I hadn't talked to him since last night because I wasn't feeling good. So, it didn't surprise me that he answered on the first ring.

"What's up? You good? Need anything?" he asked, instantly making me nervous. I didn't want to break the news to him over the phone. This was a conversation that needed to be handled face to face.

"Yes, I'm fine. Are you busy? I need to talk to you,"

"Nah, I'm not doing shit. Where you at? I can come over."

I felt the urge to throw up, but I ignored it.

"I'll send you the address."

"Aight," he ended the call and I just stood there in the middle of my kitchen. I hadn't talked to Tristan in a couple of days, but if he found out that I was pregnant by Mega, I know he's going to have a problem with it.

He still has yet to tell me why he doesn't like Mega, so I just left it alone. It didn't have anything to do with me, anyway.

After I sent Mega the address, I went to my room to shower and change. Just because I was feeling like shit didn't mean I had to look like it too. I didn't want Mega to see me looking a mess. It was a little too early for all that.

I had no idea what I wanted to wear. Having a closet full of clothes was actually pretty hard. I would stand in the same spot for thirty minutes trying to decide on what to wear.

"This is so stupid," I muttered, pulling out a long, pink, satin dress. Now that I was looking at it, I didn't really care for it. It wasn't a body hugging dress or anything, it was just plain and pink. It kind of reminded me of a night gown.

I sucked it up and put the dress on. It didn't look too bad on me. I was just glad it wasn't hugging my body. I ran my fingers through my hair, then made my way back downstairs. I didn't look like I was sick, but I surely felt like it.

As soon as I sat down on the couch, there was a knock at my door. I felt my heart rate speeding up. I was terrified to break the news to him. Who knows how he would react.

I opened the door and smiled at him. He had his hair in two braids going straight back. He stepped in the house and pulled me close to him.

"You don't look sick," he said, giving me a soft kiss on my forehead.

"I feel terrible, though. I can't eat or keep anything down," I let him know as we moved to the couch.

"Damn. Sounds like you got a stomach bug."

"Close, but no."

"What? You got the flu or some shit? If you do, I need to take my ass home."

"No, it's not the flu either."

His brows came together in confusion. "What you got shawty? Some shit I never heard of?"

"No… I'm pregnant." I kind of just blurted the words out because that was the only way I would be able to tell him.

He was quiet for a moment. We just stared at each other, but then a big smile spread across his face.

"You for real?"

I nodded. "Yep. Just found out."

"Oh shit!" he yelled, jumping up. "You dead ass? You not playing?"

"I'm serious, Mega. You think I would call you over here and lie to you?"

He pulled me up from the couch, then started rubbing my belly. "You're carrying my babyyy," he sang, easily hitting the notes.

I looked at him through wide eyes. "I didn't know you could sing!"

He stopped rubbing tummy and looked at me. "You know, something slight. I don't ever do it, though."

"Why not? You think it's gay, don't you?"

"Nah nah. I just don't do it."

"Well, you should."

He went back to rubbing my belly without responding to me. I still wasn't sure how I felt about everything. I honestly didn't expect him to respond like that, either. I thought he would be mad... I mean, that would make me feel better about getting an abortion.

"Gonna name this little nigga Junior," he let me know.

"What? How do you even know that it's gonna be a boy? What if you have a daughter?"

"Nah, I make boys."

I giggled as he kissed me all over my face. In the small amount of time that I knew him, I'd never saw him this happy. He couldn't stop smiling and I still felt weird about it.

My life was too hectic right now for a baby. I have to worry about my family members trying to kill me, and doing that while pregnant will be so much worse. I don't want to be shooting people while I'm pregnant. I don't want to shoot anyone at all.

"So, you're okay with this?" I finally asked after a while of silence.

"Okay with what? You being pregnant?"

"Yeah... we barely know each other."

"What? I know everything about you shawty,"

I took a step away from him and crossed my arms. "No, you don't."

"I promise I do,"

"What's my last name?"

"Martin."

"How old am I?"

"Twenty-two."

"What's my favorite color?"

He chuckled and ran a hand down his face. "Yellow, shawty."

I screwed my mouth up. He was right, but how? I don't remember telling him any of that. I didn't know anything about him. I only knew that his first name was Mega.

"How though? I've never told you any of that."

"I just know everything." He gave me a small smirk.

"But I don't know anything about you. Are your parents still alive? What's your favorite color? I don't even know what you do for a living."

He sat down on the couch, but made sure to bring me down with him. I felt nervous sitting in his lap like I was a high schooler.

"You don't need to know what I do for a living," he said easily. "Where's the remote at?"

"Huh? Why not? I think I should know."

He shook his head. "Nah, you good ma."

"Well whatever you do, it has to be some kind of money involved because your house was really nice. Now I really wanna know what you do for a living. I know you don't work a nine to five."

"Hell no," he snapped. "You won't ever catch me working for the white man."

"You sell drugs, don't you?"

"What? Nah, I don't do no shit like that."

I lifted an amused brow because honestly, that's what I thought he did. Now, I didn't know. I never see him go to work and I never hear him talking about work.

"So, you just sit on your butt all day and make money?"

He shook his head with a small smile on his face. "I'm a killer. I kill people for a living."

I laughed and lightly hit him on his chest. "You're so silly."

"I'm dead ass." He let me know, causing my laughter to stop.

"So, you're like a hit man?"

"I guess you can call it that."

He was so nonchalant about it. Now, I really didn't know how to feel. My child's father killed people for a living.

"Oh goodness," I muttered to myself. This was all too much to take in right now. I just needed to go back to sleep and try it again tomorrow.

19

ALAYA

"Girl no. That nigga is crazy." I said to my friend Junni as she sat on my couch.

"All the niggas you fuck with are crazy. How's he any different?"

"Okay, so I go over there because he claims he was gonna cook for me, but his house started getting shot up and shit! I go downstairs and his cousin standing over a dead body. That bitch really shot a woman and they both acted like the shit was normal. What the hell kinda shit?"

"Wait," she laughed. "Who the hell was the woman that got killed?"

"I think his cousin said something about it being his mom. I don't know. I just know the bitch was dead. I don't want no parts of that shit."

"Told you there would be something wrong with his ass. Don't know why you didn't listen to me."

"Girl, there's something wrong with all these niggas. I just need to be like you and get me a married man. Seems like y'all don't have any problems."

She chuckled lightly. "Bitch fuck you. They're in the process of getting a divorce. He just bought me a new house, too."

Junni had a sugar daddy. She wouldn't call him that, but that's exactly what he was. Junni didn't even have to work because that nigga stayed giving her ass money.

"I bet he did. Shit, tell him to get me a house too. I'm tired of paying bills up in this shit."

"Bitch, find your own," she laughed. "Maybe you should fuck with Tristan. Sounds like he has money."

"No thanks," I said, shaking my head. "I like my life. I'm not ready to die yet."

"Well, I don't know what to tell you. I didn't go out looking for Shamar. We just kinda happened."

I rolled my eyes. The only thing with that was he was married. She claimed that him and his wife were about to get a divorce, but she's been saying that since they first got together about a year ago. He was just telling her what she wanted to hear because he wasn't leaving her ass.

"So, what are you going to do when he doesn't divorce his wife again? Wasn't he supposed to do that like last year?" I asked as she flipped her hair from her shoulder.

"You can't divorce someone overnight, Alaya."

"Yeah, I know that but, they're still living together too. I thought usually when someone is getting divorced, they don't live together. Maybe you should ask them about that."

"He's at my house every night. I know for a fact he's not still having sex with her."

"True," I said, keeping what I was really thinking to myself. That man was still sleeping with his wife. He was probably just telling Junni he was at work when he was really with his wife and vice versa.

"Have you heard from Dez lately?" She asked, causing me to roll my eyes.

"Girl, that nigga calls me every damn day. That shit so annoying. Did I tell you how I came home one day and he was just in here waiting on me? I had to fight his ass, then threaten him with my brothers so his ass would leave."

"What? That nigga put his hands on you again?"

I nodded. "Sure did. He slapped my ass as soon as I walked in. Then on top of that, he busted my fuckin' nose with his gun. I should still tell my brothers because I'm tired of his ass. We're not even together."

"That nigga annoying as hell. We should get him set up or something."

I lifted an eyebrow as I looked at her. "Huh? I thought you were done with that part of your life. I haven't talked about you setting a nigga up in a long ass time."

"I mean, it was just a suggestion. You know I need some excitement in my boring ass life." She shrugged.

"Boring?" I scoffed. "Bitch, you're out here living lavish. You don't have to lift a finger because your sugar daddy does it all for you."

"He's not my sugar daddy," she let me know. "And that's exactly why my life is boring. He does everything."

I waved her off. "Nah," I laughed. "That nigga done moved you into that big ass mansion, in that white ass neighborhood and you're over there missing the hood."

"Girl bye. I don't miss nothing from the hood." Yeah, her mouth said one thing, but I could tell she was lying.

Junni was a hood bitch at heart. There were so many things we used to get into when we were teenagers. People hated when me and Junni got together. We would wreak havoc everywhere we went.

"Yes, you do. You can take the bitch out the hood, but you can't take the hood out the bitch."

"Fuck you," she laughed. "The hood stayed lit, though. There was never a boring moment."

"Exactly. Now, you wanna set a nigga up because you're bored and shit."

She smacked her lips. "Don't sit here and act like you don't miss doing hood rat shit."

"What? Nah, I'm still doing it. You're the one who got with a married man and decided to turn your life around."

"Being with an older man makes me want to act more mature."

"For what, though?" I asked, watching my phone light up on the table. "Deep down, that's not the real you. Why you tryna change for a man who doesn't even plan on leaving his wife? That don't make no damn sense."

"One day, if you ever get a man, you'll understand it." She winked at me.

"Bitch, fuck you. I can get a man easily. I just don't want one. They all come with dumb ass problems. I don't have time for it."

"Well, it sounds like you're gonna be single forever, then. What relationship doesn't have problems?"

I rolled my eyes to the ceiling. She always said the same shit about relationships. She was with a married man. Their relationship problems are probably a little different than a regular relationship.

"Anyways," I said, changing the subject. "Let's finish talking about what we're planning on doing to Dez tonight."

"So, we're really gonna do it?" Her eyes lit up like a kid on Christmas morning.

"Hell yeah. You brought it up, so now I'm excited about the shit. Plus, he deserves it for putting his fuckin' hands on me."

She smiled at me and nodded. "Cool. Change of plans, though. I wanna rob that nigga."

"How the fuck are we gonna do that? Run up in his house?" I asked, already having an attitude because the plan sounded stupid. I didn't have any weapons except for a small ass taser and some pepper spray. I knew for a fact Dez had guns. He carried one with him everywhere he went.

"No man. You invite him over here, and we get his ass high as fuck. I'm talking like making him pass out and shit. Then we take all the shit from him."

"Alright," I nodded. "This shit sounds pretty good. But, what the hell are we going to do after that? Let his big ass stay over here sleep? That nigga gonna wake up and know it was us that robbed him."

"Bitch, are you stupid or are you dumb? Why the fuck would we leave his ass here? As soon as we're finished, we're taking his big ass to his car, then dropping his ass off somewhere. Damn, girl. Use your brain."

"Damn. You don't gotta talk to me like that." I muttered grabbing my phone off the table because it was lighting up again.

"Well, you were acting hella dumb just now. Now stop talking about it and call the nigga. I'm trying to suck my man's dick tonight."

I twisted my mouth and looked down at my phone. Tristan had texted me a few times, but he would just have to wait. I didn't want to talk to him anyway.

"Crazy ass nigga," I muttered as I scrolled through my phone, then clicked on Dez's number. It didn't even surprise me that he answered on the third ring.

"What's up, Lay?" he asked, sending child down my spine. Not the good kind, either.

"Not shit," I said, trying my hardest not to let him hear the displeasure in my voice. "You doing anything tonight?"

"Hell nah. I'm actually glad you called. I've been wanting to come over and apologize

for what I did the last time I saw you."

"You good," I chuckled. "I'm over that shit. Come through tonight, though. I want some dick." I wanted to throw up as soon as I let the words leave my mouth, but I had to hold it together.

"Shit, say less. I'll be over there in about an hour."

I ended the call without saying anything to him, then sat back on the couch.

"Man, I can't believe I used to fuck that coke head ass nigga. There ain't no telling what he be sticking his dick in." I said, looking at Junni.

"I can't believe you were fucking him, either. But, it's not that big of a difference than you letting the white boy fuck you at that party."

I shrugged. "I don't even remember fucking him. That kinda pisses me off because I would like to know if he had good dick or not."

She shook her head. "You still don't give a fuck about your pussy being all over the internet?"

"Does it look like I care? It seems like it's bothering everyone around me, though. I keep forgetting that the shit even happened until someone brings it up. It wasn't even that serious to me."

At this point, I was ready to forget the video. So, what people saw my pussy? I used to be a whole stripper out here. Niggas were seeing my pussy every damn night. The only difference was I was getting paid for it.

"Shit, it's your life, not mine. I can't tell you how to live it. But what you need to do is go put on some clothes. You're gonna rob the nigga in your bra and panties?" she asked.

"Honestly, it doesn't even matter what I'm wearing. That nigga thinks I'm trying to fuck, anyway. Plus, do you see how good I look?"

Usually when I was home alone, I was just chilling in my underwear. I had a perfect body and I liked looking at it.

"So, what's he gonna do when he see the both of us?"

"Shit, probably nothing. We can just tell him we're having a threesome. You know that nigga ain't gonna turn down a threesome. That's like a nigga's number one fantasy."

I was too excited with what we had planned. Dez was a show off, so he always had money, jewelry, and drugs on him. I knew robbing him was about to be a decent come up.

"I'm not having sex with that nigga," she snapped with a disgusted look on her face.

"Duh, bitch. I'm not fucking him either. The plan was to get him high as fuck."

"Off what, though? Xans? I know you got some in here because you're a fuckin' pill head."

"Shut the hell up. I'm not a damn pill head, but I might have some laying around here somewhere. I think I wanna crush them up and make him drink it."

She nodded. "Hell yeah. That shit sounds perfect."

I smiled and made my way into the kitchen. Junni followed behind me, probably just as excited as I was.

"After we rob him, we should run through his car, too. He might have even more shit in there." I said, getting the whiskey from the freezer.

"Girl, you know damn well he's gonna have shit in his car. You know he's a dumb ass."

She was right about that. Dez was the dumbest nigga I knew. I was shocked his ass didn't get robbed more.

"Hell yeah," I laughed, crushing up the pills. Once I was finished, I poured it into the whiskey and gave it a small shake.

"We're not drinking that, are we?" she asked, causing me to look at her with the ugliest expression on her face.

"Bitch no. I'm not drinking at all. I need to be focused for this. If we mess up, I'm gonna be pissed."

"Well why you put that shit in the entire bottle? What if I wanted to take a shot or two? You didn't even ask."

"Girl, shut up. You can take a shot later. You're acting like this whiskey is the only liquor I have in my house. You should know me better than that by now."

"What if I wanted some whiskey, though? You rude as hell. I would've offered you some before I laced it with drugs."

I ignored her and walked back into the living room. The only thing left to do now was wait for his ass to get here.

"We definitely need to invest in some guns," Junni said, coming to sit down, too. "How we about to rob a nigga and we don't even have any weapons?"

"All I got is a taser and some pepper spray." I said, beginning to roll a blunt.

"What? That ain't gonna do shit. We're better off fighting him if shit gets outta hand."

"Nah, my taser will take his big ass down. Shit, pepper spray will too. If shit gets ugly, I think we'll be okay."

"If you say so." she said to herself.

About thirty more minutes went by, then Dez finally showed up. When I opened the door, he was standing there already looking high as fuck. This was perfect.

He was wearing an all-white Adidas tracksuit with hella chains on looking stupid as hell. He had gold rings on all of his fingers, and he had the nerve to have a grill in his mouth, too. The sight of him made me want to throw up, but I couldn't. Not until his ass passed out.

He lustfully eyed my body, but I didn't even blame him.

"What's up?" he asked, licking his lips.

"Hey," I smiled, stepping to the side to let him in. He smelled like he poured the entire bottle of cologne on him. Shit made me want to gag.

"Who's your sexy ass friend over there?" he asked as I shut the door.

"That's Junni. She'll be joining us tonight. That's not gonna be a problem for you, is it?"

He looked at me, then turned his attention back to Junni.

"Hell nah," He went to sit on the couch and picked up the bottle of whiskey just like I knew he would. "Oh shit. This what y'all drinking on?"

"Help yourself," I said, sitting down next to him. The way he was smelling had me wanting to open every single window in my house.

"And you already got the blunt rolled? You always been a dope bitch." He smiled at me, and I fought the urge to roll my eyes.

"Nigga, you already look like you're high as hell." Junni said, causing him to look at her with the same smile.

"I am. I got that good weed in the car. I should've brought some in here, but I wasn't thinking about it."

That nigga was lying. He had to be high off some other shit, but I wasn't going to speak on it. It was gonna be even easier for us to knock his ass out.

"I'm 'bout to open this." he said, taking the top of the whiskey.

"Do what you gotta do," I held, picking he blunt up from the table and lighting it. "I'm about to be high as hell."

Dez took his first shot, which turned into two more. After that, he took three more, and I was staring at this nigga like he was crazy. Clearly, he didn't care about his liver. He wiped his mouth and looked at me and I passed him the blunt.

"This all y'all doing? You don't got any xans or anything?" he asked. Y'all see this shit? He was a straight drug addict.

"Nope. I'm done with pills," I lied. "I'm trying to get my life together."

"What? Since when? Since that video of you went viral? Now all of a sudden, you wanna get ya life together. Yeah, okay." he scoffed, taking a pull of the blunt.

I bit the inside of my cheek. It was so hard trying to be nice to this nasty ass, nobody ass nigga. I could feel Junni staring a hole in me, but my attention was on Dez. The way I was feeling, I wanted to pepper spray him now, beat his ass a little bit, then rob him, but I had to stick to the plan.

"I know you're not over there babysitting that bottle, nigga," I chuckled, changing the subject. "You took like three shots. I just knew you were about to kill that bottle."

He looked at the bottle in his hand, then passed the blunt to Junni. "Man, I was hitting the blunt. I'm about to kill this whole bottle, though. Y'all didn't want any did y'all?"

I shook my head. "No. I just wanna smoke tonight. I don't feel like being too fucked up."

He nodded and took the bottle to the head exactly how I wanted him to. I could feel myself wanting to smile, but I suppressed it. This nigga was drinking the whiskey like it was water.

When he was more than halfway done with the bottle, he sat it down and looked at me.

"Ayo, what the fuck is this shit?" he slurred. "I'm fucked up right now, and I ain't even drink that much."

"It's regular whiskey. Don't tell me you can't handle no whiskey now," I laughed, causing Junni to laugh too.

"Nah, nah. Don't be tryna play me like I'm a bitch." He picked the bottle up again and turned it up. "Fuck," he muttered, sitting the bottle down. He started fanning himself, and when I looked at his ass, he was sweating bullets.

"Nigga, you about to throw up?" I shrieked.

"Nah. I'm good. I don't throw up." No sooner than the words left his mouth, he threw up all over my fucking floor.

"Man, hell nah!" I yelled, standing up. The sight of throw up made me want to throw up. If I threw up right now, everything would turn out bad.

Dez tried to get up from the couch, but ended up falling face first right in the throw up.

"Swear to God, I'm about to be sick," Junni said.

"I think he's gone, though." I whispered, slowly making my way over to him. I kicked him in his side and he didn't budge. That's when the smile spread across my face and I looked at Junni.

She wasted no time coming over to him and pulling all the rings off his fingers. I ran through his pockets. He had hella money in both pockets.

"Yo, this nigga dumb as hell," I laughed, pulling his car keys from his pockets. "Come on bitch."

We ran outside and went straight for his car. That nigga had hella weed just sittin' in the passenger seat. If he would've gotten pulled over trying to make it to my place, it would've been over for him.

"Look bitch," Junni said holding up two guns. Don't ask me the name of them because I had no idea.

"Good. We're definitely gonna need that shit."

I opened the glove compartment and there was even more money in there. I swear, this nigga went everywhere with all the money he had on him. The shit was crazy as fuck to me.

When we were done going through his car, we came out with hella money, hella weed, and we found three more guns. Why would he be driving around with all this shit? It didn't make any damn sense to me.

Me and Junni made it back in the house and we stood over Dez, wondering how the hell we were gonna get his big ass out of my house.

"He stinks," she said. "He smells like ass, but then it's like he tried to cover it up with all that damn cologne. What the fuck is that?"

"The nigga probably dirty," I chuckled, trying to flip his ass over. "Help me flip him. He has those chains on, which will probably cost a lot."

"No," she damn near yelled, twisting her face up. "That nigga got throw up all over him."

"Bitch, help me!"

It took everything in us to flip his big ass over but when we did it, I held my breath and snatched his chains one by one. I had to quickly look away from him because I was about to throw up. The smell was really getting to me.

My phone started ringing on the table and I got it. I blew out a breath when I saw it was only Tristan calling.

"What the fuck?" I muttered. I slid my finger across the phone and answered it. "Hello?"

"Yeah, I'm outside."

"Huh? Why?" I ran over to the window to look, and sure enough, Tristan's car was out there.

"You didn't get my texts? I told you I was about to slide through."

Fuck, fuck, fuck.

"Shit. Tristan, right now is a bad time. I um—"

"Man, open the damn door shawty? This shit unlocked?"

Before I could even say anything, the door was opening, and Tristan was stepping in. I didn't know what to say or do, so I just stood there looking at him with my mouth hanging open.

"Damn, what y'all got going on?" he asked, with his eyes darting from me to Junni. Then, they landed on Dez.

"I tried to tell you it was a bad time." I said, voice barely above a whisper.

"You should've replied to my messages, then. You had me thinking it was all good to come through and shit. What the fuck y'all got going on?" he asked again.

"Umm..."

Damnnn, why was this nigga here? I didn't know what to say to him. He's probably about to feel some type of way if I told him what was really going on.

"Y'all about to have an orgy or some shit? This the type of shit you like?" The displeasure played out all over his face.

"Nigga, no," I snapped. "I told you it was a bad time. Why didn't you listen?"

He glared at me for a moment before a small smile spread across his face.

"Y'all robbing this nigga, ain't y'all?"

How did he even know that shit? Dez could've been one of our friends, and he just passed out because he got too drunk.

"Something like that," I muttered, making my way back to Dez. Junni helped me as we tried to lift his big ass up again.

"For what? What that nigga do to deserve some shit like this?" Tristan asked, watching us struggle.

"He's done a lot to deserve this. Nigga even put his fuckin' hands on me like he didn't have any damn sense. He deserves all this shit."

"And you called me crazy?" he chuckled, folding his arms.

I looked up at him. "Nigga, you are crazy. Everything that comes with you is crazy. Like, the way you just showed up here without me responding to your texts. Crazy, bruh."

"Nah, I'm not crazy. My life is. But, that's exactly why I came over here because we need to talk."

"Right now is not a good time. Tristan!"

He shrugged. "Well, I'm not going nowhere until we talk, so."

Was this nigga serious? All I wanted to do was get Dez's ass outta here so I could go on with my night. I wasn't even surprised that Tristan was standing here, refusing to leave.

"Alright. Since you don't wanna leave, then help us get this big ass nigga to the car."

Tristan shook his head. "Nah. That nigga got throw up all over him. I'm not touching that shit."

"Then move, nigga! Fuck you just standing there for?"

It took forever, but me and Junni finally got Dez's ass to the car. I thought I was going puke from the smell, but I held it together.

"Go get my keys off the table," I told her. "Follow me in my car. I'ma drive his."

"You're not gonna put clothes on?"

I sighed to myself. "I mean, I wasn't. Ain't nobody gonna see me."

"Could you please?"

I shook my head. "No man! Go get the keys so we can be done

with this shit!" As I was yelling at her, Tristan came out the house with my keys already in his hand. I rolled my eyes as he walked over to us.

"Lemme ride with you," he said, tossing my keys to Junni. I didn't even protest. I just got in Dez's car, and Junni went to get in mine. Tristan sat in the passenger seat and twisted his face up, probably because of the smell.

"What the hell is so important that you wanna talk about?" I asked, starting the car and pulling off.

"Shittt," he said pulling a hand down his face. "I don't even know where to begin, shawty."

"I mean, you could begin with what the hell happened at your place that day. You always got people shooting at you like that?"

"Nah… They weren't shooting at me. They were shooting at Semaj."

Me and Semaj didn't talk much when I was over there, but she seemed like a sweet person. I was having a hard time understanding why so many people would be trying to kill her.

"For what, though? She doesn't even seem like the type to get herself into some shit like that."

"It's a long story." he sighed.

"Well, make it short."

"Her pops got killed, and he left everything in his will to her. Nigga had hella money. Cars, houses, businesses, and he left everything to her. The family is mad about it, so they're trying to kill her."

"What?" I shrieked. "But, that's not her fault. She didn't even ask for all this."

"Exactly. She's not even built for this type of life. She made sure to get out the hood and never come back. She acts white as hell, too. Shit crazy."

"I mean, she did kill someone, though. She looked like she was about to be sick."

"Yeah," he chuckled. "That was my mom."

I opened my mouth to say something, but nothing came out. So, it was his mom. But, the way he said it was like it wasn't even bothering him.

"She killed your mom?" I asked quietly.

"Yeah. She wasn't much of a mom to me, though. She hated my ass, actually."

"What? What kind of mom hates their own kids? Why didn't she just give you up for adoption or something?"

"Everything was straight until my dad left her ass. Since he didn't want her, she didn't want me. So, that's how she started treating me. I would go days without eating, be wearing the same dirty ass clothes because she wouldn't wash my shit. She would beat me for no reason. Man, the shit was crazy."

"So, what happened? Did you tell someone?"

"Hell yeah. I told my dad. After that, I moved in with his ass. My mom didn't give a fuck, though. She was just glad that I was gone. Then, she got pregnant again. Had another son who she treated like gold. I barely knew his ass."

I nodded. "So, it doesn't really bother you that she's dead?"

"Nah, not really. She came to my crib tryna kill me and Semaj. The only thing that's bothering me about the whole thing is I gotta go to the fucking funeral. Everyone's looking at me to plan the shit, but for what? She didn't give a damn about me, so why should I give a damn about her?"

"True," I said quietly. I didn't really know what to say back to him. His life was crazy. I couldn't even imagine going through anything like that because my mom was nothing like his.

"I really came to your crib to apologize, though. I know I took a little while to come over here and say something, but shit been crazy."

"Wait," I said, looking at him. "That shit happened like a month ago. Why is the funeral just now happening?"

"She was on life support. I been told them to pull the plug, but her nigga wasn't having it. So, they finally told him that she wasn't gonna make it, so he pulled the plug and now we're getting ready for the funeral."

"That's fucked up."

"Hell yeah,"

"And I also wanted to ask if you would come to this dumb ass funeral with me. I'ma need some type of support other than Semaj."

For a moment, I looked at him like he was crazy. I hated funerals. They were so sad. But, I understood that Tristan did need some support. No matter how much he acted like he didn't care about his mom dying, I knew it was bothering him.

"Yeah," I said glancing over at him. "I'll go with you."

20

TRAP

"So, you don't feel bad after you kill someone?" Semaj asked, sticking a grape in her mouth. Ever since she found out she was pregnant, all she been doing was eating.

"I mean, not really. I didn't know them, so there's no point of feeling bad about it. Plus, I'm getting paid for the shit. Feelings never get involved."

"That's crazy. I feel really bad about what I did to Tristan's mom. When she was on life support, I was really hoping she would pull through. I've been thinking about it a lot."

"Nah, don't let that shit bother you. She was tryna kill you, right?"
She nodded. "Yeah, but still—"

"Self-defense, shawty. What if she would've shot you? Then what?"
"I don't know," she shrugged. "I guess I would've just been dead."

"Exactly. She should've stayed her ass at home. Maybe she would've lived longer."

She popped the last grape in her mouth and smiled at me. "I'm really hungry."

"You've been eating since you got here, though. Keep eating like this and you're gonna be the size of a—"

"Excuse me? I'm not the one that got me pregnant. I haven't been eating for a whole week. Of course, I'm hungry."

"Man chill. What you want to eat?"

"Hot wings and pizza. Oh, and please get garlic on the crust. I've been craving garlic for so long."

"Nah," I chuckled, standing up. "Hell nah. You need to eat healthy. You can't be feeding my son all that shit."

"Eat healthy? You eat McDonalds every damn night. Your semen tastes like pennies, Mega. Don't try me with that 'eat healthy' shit. I'm starving. I want hot wings and pizza."

"I'm not the one that's pregnant." I let her know.

"And again, I'm not the one who got me pregnant. Hot wings and pizza. Let's go."

She stood up from the couch, flipped her weave off her shoulder and made her way towards the front door. She was mean as hell now, but I blamed that shit on hormones. Most pregnant women were mean. I don't think I've ever met a nice one.

"Get a side salad or some shit," I said, following behind her.

She let out a shrill laugh as she opened the door. "No thank you. Maybe tomorrow, I'll get a salad."

"And when you get heartburn from eating those hot wings, don't come crying to me, shawty. You really don't need to be eating this shit."

She looked at me and smiled, then got in the passenger seat of my car. She didn't give a fuck about anything I was saying to her. As long as she was getting her wings and pizza, she was good.

"The cologne you're wearing is making me sick," she let me know, rolling down her window.

"I'm not wearing any cologne. All I have on is deodorant."

"Well, it smells terrible. I hate it."

I glanced over at her. "I've been wearing the same deodorant since we met. Now, all of a sudden it's a problem?"

She nodded. "Yes, Mega. Could you roll down your window please? I would hate to puke all over your car again."

I chuckled and rolled down my window. "You crazy, Semmy."

"I really wish you would stop calling me that."

"And I wish you knew how to suck dick better, but you don't ever hear me complaining."

Her mouth fell open as she looked at me. "My dick sucking skills are great, Mega. And you don't be complaining when you cum in five minutes. Or, are you just a minute man?"

"You know damn well I'm not a fuckin' minute man. You're the one that's always tapping out. My vagina hurts," I said in a high-pitched voice. "You say that shit every time, right?"

"I do not! I can't believe you're sitting here lying like that." She looked down at her ringing phone and declined whoever was calling her. That was the third time she'd done that shit today.

"Who the fuck is that calling you?" I questioned, watching her roll her eyes.

"That guy Marcus. I'm not sure why he keeps calling me. It's a little annoying."

"Why haven't you blocked that nigga? You tryna talk to him?"

"What? No. I just didn't think to block him."

"Aight," I nodded. "Block his ass."

"Fine," she sighed.

The rest of the ride was quiet. At first, I thought she had an attitude because I told her to block that square ass nigga, but when I looked at her, she looked like she was trying to prevent herself from throwing up.

"You good? You sure you still wanna eat this?"

"Yes. I'm starving." she said, popping her door open and stepping out.

"You better eat all this shit too," I said walking behind her.

"Shut up. I'll eat until I'm full. If I don't finish it, I'll just save it for later."

I chuckled. "You're probably gonna throw it right back up. Don't even know why you're bothering to eat this shit—"

"So, what? I still need to eat. Maybe if your deodorant didn't smell so bad, I wouldn't be sick right now." She shrugged lightly and I opened the door for her.

"My deodorant smells good, girl. You trippin'."

"It really doesn't. I need you to get in the shower as soon as we get back to your place."

"What? I already took a shower today, shawty."

"There's nothing wrong with taking more than one shower in a day. The cleaner, the better."

"Aight. I'll take a shower if you take it with me."

She gave me a small smirk, then went to stand in line. "You're always being so nasty," she giggled. "I'll take one with you if you rub my feet right after."

"I'll do more than rub your—"

"What's up, nigga?" Spazz said, approaching us. "You out here looking like you're in a happy ass relationship."

I laughed as I dapped him out. "Get the fuck outta here, nigga. I should've known yo' ass was gonna be here, as much as you eat hot wings."

He looked from me to Semaj, then his eyes lit up and shit.

"Semaj? Nigga, this your girl?"

"Yeah," I said, with my eyebrows coming together. "You know her?"

"Hell yeah, we used to live next to each other."

Semaj gave him a small wave. "Hi, Spencer."

Of course, she calls this nigga by his first name. It was like she had a problem with nicknames and shit.

"I'm sorry about what happened to your pops," he said, giving me a look.

"Yeah. It's life, I guess. Everything happens for a reason."

They talked for about two more minutes before he finally decided to leave. I didn't know if I was trippin' or what, but Spazz was a little too excited for me when he was talking to Semaj. It was like he was seeing one of his old exes or something.

"Y'all used to fuck or something?" I asked, as we moved up in the line.

"No," she said, waving me off. "We were just neighbors back when my mom was still alive."

"You sure? That nigga was looking at you like he was ready to risk it all."

"Gross," she laughed. "You should've seen him back in the day. He was ugly and nerdy. Definitely wasn't my type."

"You don't even know what your type is, shawty. You said I wasn't your type, too. Remember that shit?"

"You're not, shawty," she said, trying to sound like me, but just ended up sounded country as hell. "I think you put a spell on me or something."

"Nah, I put that dick on you." I licked her ear, and she turned to look at me through wide eyes.

"Stop it, Mega. We're in public."

"The fuck that gotta do with anything?"

"A lot. I don't want anyone thinking I'll just have sex in public places."

"Ain't nobody thinking about you, but me."

It felt like we stood in that damn line for another fifteen minutes, but we finally got our food, then we were on our way back to my crib.

"I really don't wanna go to this funeral tomorrow. I'm sure it's gonna end just like my dad's did. Plus, I feel like everyone is gonna know I'm the one who killed her." she said, running her fingers through her hair.

"Nah, you're overthinking. Ain't nobody gonna mess with—"

"Yes, they are! They're gonna know that she tried to kill me, but I ended up killing her instead. What if I go to jail? Then what? I'm going to be pregnant and in jail. I don't wanna have a baby in jail."

"Chill man. You want me to come with you?"

She shook her head. "You and Tristan don't get along. I don't need y'all two fighting, either."

"I'm not gonna fight that nigga. I'll wait till after the funeral to do that shit." I chuckled.

"Could you not? Why can't y'all just drop whatever beef y'all have for me?"

"It's more complicated than that, Semmy."

"I'm sure it's really not, though. Me and you are having a baby. Sooner or later, you two are going to have to get along."

I shook my head. "Fuck I gotta get along with that nigga for? That's your family, not mine."

She smacked her lips. "What if you had a sister, and me and her were trying to kill each other all the damn time? That would upset you, right?"

"Nah. That shit ain't none of my business."

"Mega!"

"What? It's not. Just like the shit between me and your cousin is none of your business."

"That's so messed up, but whatever. No, you're not coming to the funeral since you wanna be childish," she scoffed.

"How the hell is that being childish?" I asked, watching her roll her eyes.

"Just drop it, Mega."

"Nah, answer my question. How is that being childish? You can't be mad at me because I don't like a nigga."

"I'm not telling you to like him. I'm telling you to drop the beef for me. Can you imagine how I would feel if y'all two killed each other? Now, I'm stuck raising a baby by myself because you wouldn't drop it. Then what? I'm going to eventually move on and find me a new man to—"

"You got me fucked up," I let her know. "I will come back from the dead and fuck you up if you have another nigga around my baby."

She let out a loud sigh. "I don't even know why I try to talk to you." She shook her head. "Maybe, I'll just tell Tristan that I'm not feeling good so I won't have to go to the funeral."

I glanced over at her. "You're really that scared to go to this funeral, Semaj?"

"Yes! I don't know about you, but being in a room full of people who are trying to kill me isn't something that I like doing."

"I promise you, no one is going to fuck with you."

"I know they're not. I'm not going. I'm sure Tristan isn't going to be too mad. I'm pregnant, so it's believable."

"Do whatever makes you happy." I said as she nodded.

"But, if I don't go, then it's gonna look hella suspicious. Oh my goodness," she sighed, leaning back in the seat. "My life is way too stressful."

I laughed to myself. "If you feel like that, then you might as well stay yo ass at home. I don't need you stressing out my baby and shit."

"It's so funny how you keep referring to our baby as your baby. Like you're gonna be the one who gets fat or push them out of your vagina."

"If it wasn't for me, you wouldn't even be pregnant right now. I'm the one who did this, so yeah. He's my baby."

"Men logic is so stupid," she snickered.

When we finally made it back to my crib, she ate her food like she hadn't eaten anything in weeks. I'd never witnessed a woman eating like that.

"Damn, Semmy. Maybe you should slow down. That food ain't going nowhere. You over there eating like two grown ass men and shit."

"You're really mean," she said, wiping her hands and mouth. "Instead of calling me fat all the time, you should be making me feel like I'm the most beautiful girl in the world."

"You right, shawty. Why don't you take off all your clothes so I can see how beautiful you really are."

"Actually," she yawned. "I'm so tired. I kinda wanna take a nap."

"Man, what? After I stood in that long ass line with you so you could eat? I think I deserve some pussy."

She smiled at me and stood up. "Fine, but this time, I'm getting on top first."

I didn't have any problems with that. I stood up and followed her to the bathroom. There wasn't anything else that needed to be said.

21

SEMAJ

"So, you're not going to the funeral?" Trinity asked. I was laying in Mega's huge bed, talking to her on the phone.

"Nope. I told Tristan the baby had me feeling sick. He told me it was probably for the best I didn't come anyway."

"Well, that's good. I didn't want anyone shooting at you while you're carrying my niece or nephew anyway. You still at Mega's?"

"Yes. I'm probably gonna leave soon, though. I have no idea where he went. He just left me here."

The phone went quiet for a moment.

"So, have you told him yet? How you're really feeling about being pregnant?"

I sighed to myself. "No. I haven't. He's so happy about having a baby. I don't wanna hurt his feelings or anything."

"You still need to tell him, though. Maybe he'll be okay with it."

"I can tell you right now that he's not gonna be okay with it. All he talks about is this baby. I got the abortion pills in my purse. I get nervous every time I look at them."

The other day, I went to the abortion clinic, just to see if it would make me chance how I felt about being pregnant. It didn't, though. I still feel like I'm not ready, and I don't wanna bring a baby into this situation that I'm in. Mega killed people for a living. This wasn't how I pictured having my first kid would be.

"Girl, throw those damn pills away. If you get nervous when you look at them, you know damn well you're not gonna take them. Just throw them out before Trap can see them."

"I don't know. I don't wanna have a baby. The timing is just bad." I sat up in bed and glanced around his room. His house was huge. I think there were rooms in here that I didn't even know about.

"I think you should just tell him, Semaj. If he's mad, then so what? You can help how you feel."

I nodded as if she could see me. "True, but I really don't like people being mad at me."

"So, you'd rather force yourself to have a baby you're not sure you want then have Trap mad at you for a few days? You crazy, girl."

I let out a loud breath. I still didn't know what to do.

"I saw Spencer yesterday," I let her know.

"What? Where? I forgot about that nigga. Honestly, I thought he fell off the face of the earth or something."

"I was with Mega when I saw him, too. Then Mega asked if me and him used to have something going on."

She let out a loud laugh. "Bitch, what'd you say?"

"I told him no! They were friends, Trinity. You know what that would make me look like? Mega would probably be so mad if he found out me and Spencer messed around."

"Messed around? Girl, that nigga took your whole virginity. Y'all were in love with each other. I was shocked when you broke up with him."

I rolled my eyes. "I didn't break up with him. You can't break up with someone that you're not even with."

I guess you could say Spencer was my first love. I knew him because he lived right next door, and we would hang out all the time. He was nerdy back then. He had braces, glasses that were way too big for his face, and his hair was always in a large curly fro. That's when I liked him the most. When he was Spencer, not Spazz.

At first, we just started off as friends. He would come over almost every day, but when my mom would be doing drugs, I would be over there with him. I don't remember ever seeing his mom or dad. He was living with his older brother, and he was struggling to make ends meet.

I remember how he started changing. He would always ask me weird questions about robberies, running in people's houses, and making fast money. At that time, I honestly wasn't worried about making money. I was only worried about finishing school.

It started when he got his braces off. He looked even better without them, and he knew that. Then, after the braces, he cut his hair so now, it was low and curly. He started wearing contacts, and diamond earrings, and that was it. You couldn't tell Spencer shit.

Being that me and him were just friends, I couldn't really say anything when he would be hanging out with other girls, and stuff. But, it bothered me. I don't think I've ever been so jealous before in my life. He stopped giving me attention all together because girls were all in his face now.

He went about two months without talking to me, then one random day, he saw me walking to the corner store and pulled up next to me in his car. He was seventeen and I was sixteen. I didn't even know where he got the money to get himself a car. I didn't ask any questions, though. When he told me to hop in, that's exactly what I did.

We argued a little because I wasn't feeling how he wasn't giving me his attention anymore, but after that, we spent the entire day together like we used to do. He took me wherever I wanted to go and bought me something to eat. Next thing I knew, he was taking my virginity in his bed, while his older brother was in his room sleeping.

Me and Spencer became inseparable after that. No, we never made anything official, but I was loyal to that boy like we were in a relation-ship. I thought he was being loyal to me too, but I should've known better. He was cute, getting money, and he had women basically throwing themselves at him.

He loved telling me that we weren't in a relationship. You think I would've started doing my own thing, too but I didn't. I was in love with him. I couldn't leave him alone. I refused to leave him alone. I was so dumb for him, but I think we've all been through a dumb stage.

Everything was good. Well, good enough for me to say the least. That was until one night, he had me and a couple of friends over. Things got a little heated and he started arguing with one of his boys. One thing led to another, and Spencer pulled out a gun I didn't even know he had and shot and killed his friend.

After that, I was done with him. I think the part that bothered me the most was he didn't have an ounce of remorse in his eyes. He didn't care that he had just killed someone in front of me. So, I cut him completely off. I avoided him at all costs until he finally got the hint. About a week later, him and his brother moved from those apartments, and I hadn't seen or heard from him since.

"It's so crazy that him and Trap are friends. You should've told him about y'all, though. What makes you think Spencer isn't going to tell him that y'all used to fuck? You didn't think about that, did you? Now, that nigga is gonna think you're trying to hide something from him. It's gonna be a big mess." she said, not making me feel better about anything.

"I think I'm about to head home and get my thoughts together. I'll call you later." I

"Okay, baby. I'll probably come see how you're doing later."

"Okay." I ended the call and began to put my clothes on. My body was beyond sore. I had never had sex like this. You'd think I'd be used to it by now, but nope. Mega us always trying something new, and I'm always paying for it the next day.

After I had my clothes on, I slid my way into my shoes, then headed downstairs to grab my car keys. I'd just call Mega later and let him know that I wanted to be home.

I grabbed my car keys from his kitchen table, but there was something that caught my eye. There was a manila folder lying on the table, but from the looks of it, a picture of someone that looked really familiar was hanging out.

"What the hell?" I muttered, opening the folder.

It was my dad. Pictures of my dad living his everyday life. My brows came together in confusion as I picked up the paper the had his name on it. It had all of his information on it from his businesses to the whereabouts of his houses. My heart rate sped up as I saw another piece of paper that had my name and information on it as well.

Suddenly, it was getting a little hard to swallow. My breathing was becoming shallow, and I started to feel dizzy. This was how Mega knew everything about me. He was the one who killed my dad.

"Nah," I chuckled, trying to mentally convince myself that this was probably a coincidence.

So, he knew this whole time? He knew that he killed my dad, but still talked to me like everything was normal? This man got me pregnant, knowing he killed my dad. Mega was the reason my life went to shambles. He was the reason my entire family was trying to kill me. It was all his fault.

My decision to have an abortion just got easier. I dug in my purse and pulled out the pills. What I should do is take the pills right now, in his kitchen.

I fumbled with the pill bottle top until it opened. Just as I got the pills open, the front door open. I didn't expect Mega to come home so soon. Trying to close the pill bottle, I ended up dropping the entire bottle, causing the pills to fall all over the floor.

"Shit," I hissed to myself. "Shit, shit shit."

I wasn't ready to see Mega. I wasn't ready because honestly, I didn't know what I might do to him. We were in a kitchen, and there were so many things I could use to kill him.

"What you doing just standing here?" he asked, stepping on the pill bottle by accident. He picked it up and read it. "What the hell are these?"

I glared at him. I wanted to fight him, but what would fighting do?

He didn't fight my dad, did he? Nope. He just killed him. Didn't even give my dad a chance to fight.

"Abortion pills." I let him know, watching his facial expression chance.

"Abortion pills? You gonna kill my baby?"

"Yep. Just like you killed my daddy, nigga."

TO BE CONTINUED...

HAVE YOU GRABBED THIS YET?

HAVE YOU READ THIS YET?

CPSIA information can be obtained
at www.ICGtesting.com
Printed in the USA
LVHW04s1657160618
580974LV00012B/602/P